BLOOD-RED RESOLUTION

BLOOD-RED RESOLUTION

Being Excerpts from the Crypto-Coded Files of the United Courier Service

A Novel of Adventure

by

WILLIAM MALTESE

The Borgo Press
An Imprint of Wildside Press

MMVII

CONTENTS

PROLOGUE

IT WAS TWELVE-TEN A.M., and Dayklan Incorporated's newly-launched *Spaceborn Imaging Satellite (SIS)* rose over the eastern horizon. What its electronic payload was programmed to see, record, and relay, it saw, recorded, and relayed, despite the fog at ground level.

Unluckily, for those scientists monitoring on the planet's surface, the competition's SIS had made this very same pass sixteen months before, which meant The Mentlic Group had already mapped, and acted upon, whatever the mineral resources as detected, color-coded, and spewed out on read-outs from the banks of computer link-ups below.

BLOOD-RED RESOLUTION, BY WILLIAM MALTESE

CHAPTER ONE

DANE WILCOX SET HIS TRAVEL CLOCK for a one-thirty A.M. alarm, and he dozed until seconds before the buzzer went off.

At the Machu Picchu hotel sink, he splashed his face with water that he wouldn't drink on a bet. He paid little notice to his mirror-reflected black hair, black eyes, dimpled cheeks, and cleft chin, which all came together in a rugged boyishness that belied his thirty-two years. He was no more immune than the next guy to the good-looks of other people, but he'd always considered his own physical attractiveness a superficiality.

He bundled up in a llama-wool vest that he'd bought in Cuzco. He exited his room quietly and made his way through the deserted lobby and out the front door.

Well-honed reflexes told him, without seeing or hearing other evidence, that he wasn't alone. The adrenaline, spontaneously released throughout his system, produced an attractive flush and a sheen of sweat that high-lighted the contours of his cheeks and jaw line.

"I'm sorry," she apologized. "I thought you saw me."

Saw her? Did she think he was a bat?

She sat in the dark, not even the glow of a cigarette to say *here I am*. People weren't so easily spotted since the link between smoking and cancer had
re-popularized chewing gum.

She was lucky he hadn't blown her and her chair
right off the patio and over the escarpment. Dane
had reached for his SIG 49. Only intuition had
stopped him. This wasn't, after all, an official battle
zone. Someone out here, even at this time of night,
didn't necessarily mean *beware the enemy*.

"Did I look startled?" he asked.

"Are there extensive Inca ruins on this mountaintop?" she answered indirectly. Her accompanying laugh was low and throaty. A smoker's laugh,
before cigarettes became more dangerous than
sticks of dynamite. Sexy.

Dane's eyes were better adjusted; it was no
longer as dark as it had originally seemed. There
was a luminescence to the fog overflowing the
Urubamba Gorge. Whiffs of vapor danced here and
there, disappeared to materialize in different places
and shapes. Moisture pinpricked his skin. Here were
all the ingredients every spook flick could have
asked for, and more.

The woman was blonde and well-tanned. No
spotlights needed to tell any of that. She had nice
legs, too; they were encased in tight-fitting trousers,
the cuffs of which were tucked into shiny black riding boots.

"I assumed I was the hotel's only insomniac,"
Dane excused his late-night appearance on the patio.

"It's the air," she rationalized for him, "or lack
thereof. The latter knocks some people out. Oth-

ers...." She shrugged. "Maybe, between us, we tipped one cup of coca tea too many. You know the spiel? *Have one. Have two. On no account, Mr. and Mrs. Tourist-in-Peru, have three!*"

He laughed. No one had ever actually officially given *him* those de-rigueur instructions for combating altitude sickness, but it was standard fare, used by every tour escort who ever rode roughshod over every tourist group herded through Machu Picchu on an assembly-line basis, in and out in four-hours flat: poor old folk suffering from *soroche*. Gasping for breath. Asking for a bit of pure oxygen divvied up like precious elixir from portable tanks. Splitting headaches. Nausea. Saved from death only by a whirlwind schedule that had them back to lower elevations in no time.

Coca tea looked sickly green and tasted even worse than it looked; Dane never had experienced the reputed euphoria of an overdose.

She motioned to a vacant chair at her commandeered table.

He checked his watch. He didn't have the time for meaningless chit chat, or whatever. He had an appointment to keep within the pea-soup fog.

"Symptoms of *soroche* tell me I'd better hit the sack if I want to be standing in the morning," he excused.

"I would have thought you'd be acclimatized by now," she surprised. "Doesn't sickness come from being up and around one's first day in?"

He tried to read something into that. He warned himself against paranoia. It was no big deal: her knowing that he'd been at the hotel for more than one day. Any waiter could have told her; which, it turned out, had been the case.

"Pedro served me lunch today and said you'd been here *three* days. I actually made it a point to ask, since you looked too fresh for your own good."

There was *something* curiously sensual about the way she said *fresh*.

"You planning to be here for awhile?" he asked. If Roger were out there, Roger could just wait. He'd kept Dane waiting. Turnabout was fair play. This woman was far more inviting than the geologist.

"I'm hoping to stay here long enough to adjust well enough to the altitude to see the sights without an accompanying headache," she answered.

"Holiday?"

"I read this romance novel," she said. "*Beyond Machu*. Ever hear of it?"

What was she thinking! He didn't read that stuff. He'd never met a man or woman, before now, who'd willingly admit to reading it, either.

"Two men, believe it or not, Machu Picchu, and love on this very mountaintop."

"You don't say," he said lamely.

"I said to myself: *Self. I'm going there. And here I am.* Sure enough, here's a handsome man. Tell me you don't have another handsome man awaiting you in the wings."

He echoed her laughter. He couldn't help it. He didn't need genius IQ to know she was putting him on.

"Obviously, the lack of oxygen makes me giddy," she apologized.

She got up and was shorter than he'd thought. She came to his mid-chest; that made her around five-five. She extended her hand for his; no talons on this matter-of-fact lady; no bitten-to-the-quicks, either.

Suddenly, he was sorry they were parting.

Her handshake was firm. She smelled of some exotic flower. Heady stuff: her touch, her perfume, the night mist, the exotic mountain-top setting. Maybe that romance author knew something after all.

"Will I see you tomorrow?" she asked and smiled as if she'd like just that. Some women made, *I'd like a loaf of French bread, please,* sound sexy: this one had the knack.

If he didn't know her name, he had all intentions of finding out. She beat him to the punch: "Helen Mallory." It could as well have been Helen of Troy: the face and body to launch those thousand ships.

Dane would have introduced himself, but she beat him to that, too: "And you're Dane Wilcox." Her lips were pale pink. Their natural color? Her teeth were small and pearly white. Would such teeth nibble at his lips if he kissed them? "The waiter told me you were one of us *special* ones who hang around longer than the normal *in-and-out-the-same-or-very-next-day tourists.*"

Did the waiter know of Dane's nightly strolls? Was that how Helen happened to be there?

"Maybe you can spare a few minutes, come day-light, to show me around?" she suggested and let her hand stay in his until he reluctantly freed it. Her eyes sparkled and caught moonlight, or starlight—anyway, whatever the light that filtered in through the fog. Her eyes were some light color. Maybe blue, maybe green, maybe grey. "My spy tells me you've been to the high *Huayna* terraces. See any snakes along the way?"

He shook his head. "BEWARE OF SNAKES! however, *is* on one of the signs up there."

"I hate snakes," she said. "I hate spiders. I climb on a chair at the first sign of a mouse."

That had to be an exaggeration. She looked and sounded like she could take care of herself. Beautiful didn't necessarily equate with helplessness.

"I eat breakfast early," he said. "You?" He might as well make his stay—and hers—as pleasant as possible. He had nothing to do until Roger showed. *If* Roger showed; there were no guarantees.

"Starting tomorrow, *I* eat breakfast early," she said.

She smiled again and brushed by him. She left a trace of perfume; it lingered within the strands of mist set into motion by her departure.

Dane had his exit along the pathway memorized. Good thing, too, because he was late, and it was easy to walk off the edge, mistaking cloud for solid ground. A long fall. Condors could, and did, soar between him and the bottom, in clear weather looking like specks of dust in the vortex of a drain as they did so.

It was uphill to the gate where, every day, an indigenous Indian collected entrance fees. The Indian, though, disappeared when the transient tourists, at precisely two-thirty, headed down the Hiram Bingham Road to catch the three-o'clock train out of there. After that, permanent *special* hotel guests had full run of the ruins, without paying a *sol*.

There weren't that many overnighters; the rustic hotel could boast only thirty-one rooms. To coax more tourist traffic, die-hard capitalists had successfully out-lobbied conservationists for the bigger hotel whose skeletal remains were rotting on the nearby rock foundations found, too late, to be too soft to support them. Nature had triumphed where ecologists had failed.

There were times when it was easy for Dane to imagine he was alone on this mountaintop. Not a soul in sight. Not a human sound. Like now. Except, now was different, because he couldn't tell he was on a mountaintop. There was no sign of the deep hole to his right. Fog filled it, overflowed it, and piled high above it. Wet. No hint of the preceding balmy day. Sunset dropped mercury, like a lead balloon, to freezing and below.

Fog-parenthesized Inca masonry appeared on his right. It was a wall capped by thatched roof. The stones were ancient and without mortar. Thin paper couldn't be squeezed between the joints. The roof was modern: a convenience for tourists who wanted to see the ruins from cool comfort during the heat of Peruvian summers. Only die-hard archaeological enthusiasts ventured into the panoramas beyond the *rest hut*. Tonight, there were no such people and no such view.

Grass flowered droplets of distilled moisture and sprouted where foot traffic was never heavy enough to keep even this frailest of growth beaten down. The wet streaked Dane's boots and then reformed as crystal-like beads on wax-saturated leather.

He was on one of the hundreds of terraces layering the mountain. They held the top soil once carried in buckets from the valley by a now lost race of people. What once grew potatoes and maize now grew moss and weeds.

A gust of wind smacked Dane's face with a dollop of wetness. His cheeks stung from the blow. His eyes watered. This wasn't a place to be savored at night, except by a masochist. Far better by day, sunlight glinting off greens, grays, and blacks. Lovely, then. Peaceful, then. One could even imagine Incas, then, living here while Pizarro ransacked other Inca citadels and toppled Inca gods.

Now, though, it was night, and Machu Picchu was habitation more attuned to the dead than the living.

He stopped and listened. Hearing what? *Roger?*

Tonight, he actually wasn't expecting him, and he wasn't sure just why.

He heard a pebble. Freed from its matrix by water expanded-to-ice by low temperatures in some hairline crack, the stone, like a marble, cascaded from one terrace to the other, finally taking that final silent leap into the void of the gorge. No one hearing the first click of such a stone bouncing upon stone would likely hear its final shatter far, far below.

Dane reached the altar where some guides insisted Inca priests had once conducted bloody human sacrifices. Other *experts* pooh-poohed the notion. In the end, did Dane really care?

Where was Roger if he wasn't here?

Dane should have stayed with Helen. He enjoyed her company.

He was cold, and he was tired.

Another sound. No going, going, going, going, gone of a pebble this time. An *I-am-out-here* kind of noise. Roger suddenly where he was supposed to be? Helen deciding not to accept Dane's first refusal?

"Hello?" It was a line Dane borrowed from horror movies. Cue the fog. Cue the wind. Cue the monster. Cue the jerk waiting to *get his* from the mad slasher, the ax murderer, the zombie cannibal, the werewolf, the vampire, the thing from outer space or Black Lagoon. So, what would your everyday *hot-to-spend-a-few-days-at-Machu-Picchu* tourist ask in Dane's place? Assuming an everyday tourist was dumb enough to wander the fog of this potentially dangerous mountaintop at this hour of the early morning.

"Isn't there a Sandburg poem about *fog creeping in on little cat's feet*?" It was impossible for Dane to tell from where someone asked that question. The fog distorted as well as concealed.

They were playing big-boy games here, and Dane followed the rules: "I don't know if it was Sandburg." That was *his* part of the prearranged greeting/response code. "I *do* believe, though, it was cat's *paws,* not feet."

"Mind coming over this way? I've had a hard go of it."

"Keep making sounds," Dane instructed.

"La, la, la," the answer was unenthusiastic.

Dane spotted him against the Inca wall. "What in the hell happened to you? I'd guess run over by a semi if there were one within a thousand miles."

"What *didn't* happen to me?" He had a makeshift bandage around his head. It was slung low over one eye. What there was to be seen of his face was scratched and puffy. His clothes were rejects from

17

some ragbag. "We had trouble," he said; it sounded like the obvious understatement it was. "Chimchuck, I'm afraid, had even more of a bad time of it than I did. Seems we were expected."

Dane slipped off his vest, but his offer was refused. "Someone might have spotted you in that," he was reminded. "It wouldn't do for me to show up someplace wearing it."

"You won't show up anywhere, period," Dane forewarned, "if you die of exposure."

"I'm fine." His teeth chattered accompaniment. "Actually, I'm fond of the cold. No bugs, no sweat. I've had enough of both of those to last me a lifetime."

"What happened to Chimchuck?"

"As I said, *they* got him." He shuddered. "What about you? Anything suspicious at this end?"

"Not that I've noticed." Was *Helen-of-Troy-on-the-patio* something out of the ordinary?

"Well, count your lucky stars." He fished into his pants pocket for three small stones. "There were larger ones," he said, "but I ejected them, one at a time, along the way. Surprising how a mere few ounces can come to seem virtual tons after a few days of lugging them on the trail."

Dane took a good look at what he'd been handed. "So, these are what all the fuss is about." They looked as if he could have picked them up anywhere.

"It's *blood-red-resolution matrix,* nevertheless," the battered man confirmed. "A whole formation of it is laid down atop a sedimentary deposit of common garden-variety *blue.* So said the spectrometer which color-coordinated that message. By the way, if anyone asks, I abandoned the spectrometer during my hasty exit."

"What do you do now?" Dane's first guess would be *die*.

"Head down the Hiram Bingham to the train depot. Take the first train out. Might even keep them off your tail for awhile, but I wouldn't count on it. These people were not happy to see us. They were less happy to see me get away from them. You armed?"

"SIG 49."

"Danish?"

"Swiss. Nine mm."

"Just don't lose your gun. Those rocks I just gave you may look like nothing to you. They may look like nothing to me. They may *be* nothing. But there are people out there doing an awfully lot to keep Dayklan Incorporated from getting a close look-see."

Dane slipped the stones into his vest pocket.

"Sure you wouldn't like this vest?" he offered one more time. The guy didn't look as if he'd survive the night.

"You just worry about getting the merchandise to Cuzco and to Gregory."

"I could come back and pick the vest up from you before sunrise," Dane tried again.

"Look, I *do* appreciate your concern. I've just reached a point where I want to pass on this commitment and be done with it. If I never see Peru again, it'll be too soon."

"First thing I'd do, if I were you, is find a doctor," Dane diagnosed.

"And the second is take a long vacation."

Reluctantly, Dane headed back to the hotel, alone. He was brought up short by muffled sounds suddenly evident in the shadows just left behind him.

Reflexes turned him. Simultaneously, common sense warned him to get out of there before someone kicked him over the precipice.

Nonetheless, he went back.

No need to check Roger for a pulse. Dane knew death when he saw it, and this premature death could be blamed on Roger's suddenly cut throat.

Even as he contemplated the whereabouts of Roger's killer or killers, he was grabbed from behind. A rope was slipped around his neck, a knee placed firmly to his spine. There was no space for his grappling fingers between the rope and his throat.

He tried elbow jabs into hard-as-steel muscle— with little success.

He needed to access the gun he wore in the small of his back. The SIG 49 could take out an assailant bigger than this one. Trouble was, he couldn't find it.

He'd have to rely on self-defense, pure and simple.

He wanted to scream for help: there were no heroes in foxholes or at times like this. He wasn't James Bond. Nothing, however, was coming out of him but breathless gasps.

Whatever had possessed him to think he could handle this assignment?

His end was near. It didn't take long at an altitude over nine-thousand feet, where oxygen was at a premium under the best of circumstances, to give up the ghost. All it took was this chokehold held for a few seconds longer, and that was all she wrote!

He never was sure what he did, or how he did it, but he lucked out, because his attacker suddenly produced a music-to-Dane's-ears *what-have-you-done-to-me* groan.

Still alive, Dane collapsed to both knees. His spine telescoped in the process, but what was a bit more pain?

He continued his pitiful gasps for air, surprised to be alive.

He wanted and needed his gun. Too bad it had chosen that particular time frame in which to be somewhere else. Where?

He made an additional effort to pull himself together. There was no one out here to do him any favors. *He* had to take stock, make plans, execute, figuratively and literally. He'd been up against worse and had survived on more than just well-conditioned body and acute reflexes. He'd used his good old Wilcox brain, and he could use it again, if it wasn't as fucked up by oxygen deprivation as the rest of him.

Maybe his assailant never had any intentions of killing him. Maybe the attack was defensive, triggered by Dane's sudden (and unexpected?) reappearance. Maybe pigs could fly and cabbages were kings.

All he could hear was his own breathing; he held his breath. Were those disgusting sounds his? Was that more ice-loosened scree scattered by Dane's fleeing assailant? Anyone putting bets on Dane's wishful thinking?

Finally, though, it dawned on him that whoever had jumped him was gone back into the shadows. That realized, he checked for the rocks in his vest pocket.

They were still in place.

Feeling the worst for wear, he relocated Roger's body.

Roger's pockets were turned inside-out. Stones looked for but not found? To what conclusions?

Quite by accident, he literally stumbled over his gun. Had it dropped of its own volition, or been discarded by the mystery man after a skillful disarming of Dane?

Dane took more rational stock and decided he'd not come out as badly as he might have. What's more, the transfer of the stones, from Roger to him, had been successful. Score points for his side.

CHAPTER TWO

HE DIDN'T NEED TO SEE HELEN'S six-A.M. expression to know something was up.

"Have you heard?" she asked and looked even prettier in daylight; there was something decidedly favorable to be said of green-eyed blondes who tanned well.

"I'm just up and out." Dane ached in muscles he hadn't thought he had any more.

"I'm the one who found his body, can you believe it?" She shuddered. "It was *not* particularly pleasant, let me tell you."

Dane knew, without further elucidation, that his exercise in *hide-Roger's-body-until-I-can-get-out-of-here* had been for naught. He might as well have saved his time and energy. Nevertheless, he asked: "Found whom?" *Company* Couriers were given acting lessons for times just like this.

"They don't seem to know the *whom*. There's an inspector on his way from Cuzco to investigate."

"Why don't we get some coffee," Dane suggested, "and you can fill me in."

Readily, she hooked her arm with his and let him lead her to a patio table.

Dane wondered if Roger, dragged out of concealment, was now in the hotel freezer.

He motioned for a waiter (Pedro?) who was more interested in discussing events with his fellow employees than in taking another breakfast order. Dane's look expressed the opinion that coffee had better be forthcoming *or else*. That accomplished, he turned his full attention back on Helen. "Now, about this body of yours?"

"Like what you see, do you?" She sat straighter to put her already nice breasts into even better display.

"I meant the body with the...." He almost pantomimed a slit throat, but *slit throat* was far more information than he should have had at the moment. "...obvious problem."

"Oh!" Her feigned disappointment provided a sexy pout to her sensuous mouth.

"Not that *your* body has escaped my attention," he complimented.

"Thanks, but I know what I must look like this morning. What's more, I never look my best after a night like last night when I don't sleep as well as I should. Restlessness was what got me up with the chickens. Up even before the kitchen help, I strolled off to kill some time and ran across this huge bird; you know, a...." She seemed to be searching for just the right word or words to describe and convey the horror of that moment of discovery.

"A condor?" Dane suggested. Bloody scavenger probably smelled the blood before the sun even came up.

"Not that it paid *me* any mind." She folded her arms on the table and leaned across.

"Not the best way to start a morning." Dane was talking about *his* morning. He had expended a lot of time and effort to hide Roger, apparently all for nothing.

"Definitely *not* romantic," she concluded.

"So, how about some sight-seeing to take your mind off the macabre before this inspector arrives to occupy all our free time?" Dane suggested. "Although I *do* have to make a phone call, first."

"You're allowed one."

He would have called Gregory the night before, but there was no cell-phone service, and the hotel switchboard closed at nine. This morning, the latter had, likewise, been absent its operator who was chatting up, with cohorts on the verandah, the morning's unusual-to-say-the-least occurrence, until Dane insisted the woman come inside and perform the service for which she was being paid.

"Girlfriend, or wife…needing the telephone re-assurances?" Helen asked when Dane made his reappearance.

"My mother's sister's husband's cousin, actually." If the best lies were the simple ones, he was off to a bad start. "He's in Cuzco, and I promised to catch him for dinner. Your discovery of the body gave me a good reason to beg off. It wouldn't look too good, my scooting off from here, just as the inspector arrives. I suppose we're all suspects."

"Are we?" Ah, the sounds of such pure innocence!

"Not too many of us *special* ones were up here last night," Dane reminded.

"Who says the guy wasn't killed during yesterday's *turistas* swarm? I can't imagine his killer sticking around to answer questions, can you?"

Dane liked the way this woman thought.

"There aren't any trains after three," he was loathe to remind. "It's a mighty long walk out of here. Maybe the murderer didn't have any choice but to stick around."

"I can't believe anyone would be so stupid. Would you kill someone and then stick around?"

"Guess not."

"Of course you wouldn't. Neither would I. Far easier to arrive at Machu Picchu under the cover of a crowd, commit the deed, and exit under cover of the same crowd headed out on the three-o'clock train. If you ask me, this inspector is headed here after the proverbial horse is long gone through a barn door left open way too long."

"Wouldn't the dead man's tour group have missed him?" Dane played Devil's Advocate.

"Who says the dead man or his killer came with any group?"

"Are you sure it's not mysteries you read, instead of romances?" he teased her.

* * * * * * *

EVEN AFTER HIS FEW DAYS on the mountain, Dane hadn't tired of the view—in the sunlight—as he took Helen to explore some of it.

The awesome Urubamba Gorge plunged steeply and bottomed out in the rusty brown of *the-river-still-carving*. The railway paralleled the river, below, in semblance of a roadway: deceptive in that there were no roads connecting this place to civilization. The Hiram Bingham, named after the U.S. senator who discovered the Inca ruins, was an independent meander scar on the mountain, with a visible start and finish, which was used for the convenience of tourists wanting up the mountain from the station in the gorge. Before vans were shipped in by rail, it was leg-power, or the back of an ass, that was required to get the curious up top.

The name *Machu Picchu* was a misnomer, since it was the more picturesque *Huayna Picchu* that hogged all the travel posters.

Dane led Helen in a beeline toward the ancient Inca altar. She stopped him before they got there. "I've already seen enough of what's farther off that way."

"Ah, the body, you mean?" He feigned complete innocence.

"The hotel manager says it has to be left where it is until the authorities arrive. I informed him as to how there was a buzzard already destroying vital evidence, even as we spoke. He assured me someone would be sent to keep the birds away. I'd just as soon not find out if he's been true to his word." She shaded her eyes and gazed skyward. "Especially since the local condor population does seem to be off *somewhere*."

"Actually, they don't become all that active until rising temperatures provide them with enough updrafts for gliding." At the same time, Dane wondered why one greedy bird had lucked out. While he was counting his bad run of luck, he might as well add: *why had Helen picked that particular morning for a pre-breakfast stroll?*

"It is beautiful up here, isn't it?" she said. *"During the day,"* she qualified and posed on the edge of an Inca-made outcropping that overhung the valley. "Who'd ever dream any and all of this being here, last night, what with all that fog? Genuinely spooky in the dark, isn't it? Stereotypical atmosphere for a murder. Shades of *Macbeth* and all of that."

"Shakespeare, now, is it? Your reading habits *are* truly catholic."

"Well, Los Angeles isn't exactly the literary wasteland some people imagine. For every movie I saw, my parents insisted I read one book."

"Smart parents."

"Well, I won't say I thought them anything but aggravating at the time, but I've since amended my opinion. These days, I see far more of the printed page than I do of pictures on the screen."

"When you're not busy traveling, you mean?"

"This is really my very first trip of any note." She stepped back from the edge of the precipice and joined him to head other than toward the body. "Even so, I filled my suitcase with trashy best-sellers. How was I to know I'd run across that hoped-for mystery man *and* that never-expected corpse?"

Dane stepped back to let her precede him through a gauntlet of overturned stones.

Sunlight caught in her hair and provided a white halo.

He came abreast, and they walked that way for a few more yards. He would have asked what she did for a living—she seemed like a woman who could hold her own—but such an inquiry invited reciprocity. Granted, he had his *Company* cover story down pat, based on truths and half-truths, and downright lies, but he hadn't yet reached the point where falsehoods of any kind rolled off his tongue as freely and with the glibness his job sometimes—*this time*—demanded.

Helen volunteered information on herself: "I lucked out, during my sophomore year in college. Rather, between my sophomore and junior years, when I worked at a boutique where Liz Valum came around one day with some of her things." She paused—maybe expecting name-recognition but not surprised when Dane seemingly wasn't all that knowledgeable of a presently really big name in women's fashion. "I thought Liz's stuff was wonderful, but my opinion wasn't shared by the store owner, much to the owner's ultimate chagrin— especially since the owner is no longer in business, and I've just retired on my share of returns from loans I made Liz, from a small inheritance, which kept Liz from starving during some of her lean years."

"Retired, you say?" Dane was genuinely impressed. Without asking, he was sure Helen couldn't be older than twenty-nine.

"Oh, not *forever-and-ever-amen* retired," she quickly qualified. "No matter how many mystery men, romantic locales, and dead men in my life, I need something more. I just haven't decided which of several routes to go. My association with Liz is a tough act to follow, but I'm not anxious to become involved with Revlon who bought her out, although they've extended an offer. I'm more geared to one-on-one relationships. How about you?"

He'd already mentally rehearsed his spiel about running a guide service in a wilderness area of Washington State. Actually, *his brother* ran it, although their dad had legally left it to the both of them. Dane was *supposedly* in Peru scouting out the possibilities of international expansion—*à la Sobek*. In truth, his brother complained about too much business already, and Dane had no desire to baby-sit tourists to Machu Picchu or to anywhere else.

As it turned out, he was saved from immediate prevarication by the bullet that hit Helen and sent her barreling toward the lip of the gorge.

Dane dropped automatically into a crouch and drew his gun. He wasn't sure Helen wasn't, even then, airborne in the abyss until he caught a glimpse of the bottom of her foot.

"Helen?"

He got no response, so he zigged left, then right, not reassured by the sudden lack of gunfire. A barrage of slovenly aimed bullets didn't kill as readily as one very carefully aimed one. He could picture himself skillfully being lined up in some unseen gun's deadly crosshairs.

Dane would bet his paycheck from this assignment, and his *Company* pay wasn't chicken feed, that the bullet that hit Helen had been meant for him. He didn't need sophisticated computations, incorporating bullet origin, trajectory, and angle of impact, either. Having been frustrated, Dane's assailant of the night before was merely back to finish off Dane in the bright light of the new day.

"Dane?" Helen was weak-voiced.

"How badly are you hurt?" He was more distraught by her injury than by Roger having bought the farm. If he knew Helen only slightly better than he'd known Roger, she was an innocent bystander. Roger had known the risks and had taken his chances. Helen was merely a young woman on holiday. She wanted good times and good memories. She hadn't come halfway down the globe to find a dead body or become one.

"My arm is bloody," Helen diagnosed, "but I think the bullet went right through. How about you?"

"Feeling better now that I've heard from you."

"Who's shooting at us?"

"Whoever: a definite crazy," Dane identified without identifying. No need to try and explain just how he knew the shooter's real motivation. Even if Helen saw the rocks he was now carrying with him, she wouldn't believe all the fuss being made over them; Dane hardly believed the fuss himself.

"Is the shooter gone do you think?" Helen asked and sounded better than seconds before.

"Don't stand up to find out," Dane warned.

"Would you believe my mother wanted me to go to Hawaii? I told her a tanned beach-boy was not *my* idea of romantic."

"Think of the guys you can now impress with the scar you're likely to end up with from that bullet wound."

"Do, please, consider yourself welcome at the head of that line."

Someone shouted: "Hello!"

"Hello, yourself!" Dane shouted back to whom he considered one very cheeky gunman. Except....

"I think that's Mr. Candly," Helen ventured, "and I can't believe he's our shooter."

"Mr. Who?" Dane wanted to know.

"I thought I heard gunfire," Mr. Candly yelled.

Dane saw him, now. An elderly Englishman, probably in his late sixties. Prone to tweeds and a walking stick, the latter with an eagle-head handle carved from a hunk of ivory that would have had environmentalists' hackles standing on end. Distinguished looking, if anyone should ask. Right at home at a grouse hunt, even if he didn't obviously appear to have a gun. What's more, it hadn't been any sixty-year-old man who had physically taken on Dane the previous evening.

"Someone shot Miss Mallory," Dane said.

"Surely not!" Mr. Candly very well sounded as if he couldn't believe that were really true.

Mr. Candly kept standing ramrod straight. He looked this way and that: an omnipotent Wellington surveying the battlefield. Napoleon would have never found a more perfect target at any turkey shoot.

* * * * * * *

TWO HOURS LATER, Helen joined Dane at a hotel parapet. Far below, a toy-like train didn't disgorge its usual tourists. All potential sightseers had been detrained in Cuzco to make room for the inspector and his accompanying military contingent who looked ant-like as they all jockeyed to get into the vans that would bring them up the mountain.

"How's the arm?" Dane inquired of Helen.

"The hole will make a nice finger-muff on cold evenings." She offered him her drink. "I don't think alcohol goes with tetracycline."

He took her glass and sipped vodka/tonic.

How long was he going to be stuck on this mountain? There was no leaving prematurely without someone pointing a *curious-as-to-why* finger directly at his exiting tail.

"Tell the inspector, first thing, that you expect him to call in a qualified doctor to take care of your arm," Dane instructed. "Let that get infected, and you're at risk of ending up dead after all."

"And what exactly do I tell the inspector about your gun—if anything?"

Warning lights went off in Dane's head. "I've carried one ever since a grizzly tried to walk off with me at Rainier National Park, one holiday." An exaggeration, to be sure.

"I see." Convinced? "I couldn't help notice you put the gun away before Mr. Candly saw it. I thought, maybe, well...."

"You thought right." He was glad they had established enough of a rapport for her to think, now, before she acted. "The inspector will point out how there are no grizzlies in Peru." Actually, he knew of no grizzlies in Rainier Park, either.

"I wouldn't want to get you in trouble. You *were,* after all, defending me, gun-drawn. You might like to know I have no intentions of mentioning you were armed."

"Thanks." The gun was *clean,* issued out of a *Company* "store" in Cuzco, but a non-*Company* inspector would want to know how Dane got it and why.

The vans, with their newly acquired contents, began the winding drive up the hill.

"Maybe we should find you a chair?" he suggested. "You're a woman wounded, remember?"

"And mercy me, I don't think I can take one more step without a gentlemanly arm on which to lean," Helen used her best southern drawl. She batted long eyelashes over expressive eyes and smiled up at him.

They detoured around a small group of standing fellow hotel guests just as one dropped his liquor glass with a crash.

Everyone jumped like dancers of *The Time Warp* from *The Rocky Horror Picture Show*.

The guy choked. But on what? An olive? An ice cube? The *Hotel de Turistas* wasn't known for its martinis, and only a very brave man would risk the disconcerting possible medical consequences of drinking the local water—frozen or otherwise.

"Can you talk?" Dane asked. Someone choking supposedly *couldn't* talk. Ask Dane who, last night, in his grapple on that very mountaintop, had become a leading authority.

"I can't *breathe*," the guy grunted. Name of Timothy *Something-or-other*. He'd checked into the hotel immediately after Dane. He'd tried to start up a friendly conversation at the time, but Dane hadn't been anxious to get chummy with anyone.

There'd been something Timothy said, at the time, about *backpacking the Inca Road*. "I...can... not...breathe!" he repeated, louder and with more emphasis. His face went from blue to dark purple and he wobbled on his feet.

Mr. Potter, at Mrs. Potter's insistence, grabbed hold and proceeded to perform the Heimlich Maneuver, in spite of Dane's warning that you didn't necessarily use it if the subject was coherent; if you did, you risked breaking ribs for nothing. Not that Mr. Potter got in more than one quick squeeze before Timothy converted to dead-weight. Mr. Potter, not up to holding on, but reluctant to let go, collapsed right along with the man to whom he was attempting to give succor. The old man's cry of pain wasn't pretty as his knees hit hard ground *and* broken glass. Except, no one paid any attention to Mr. Potter; Timothy, the continued star of the moment, began foaming at the mouth like a rabid dog.

Dane looked for something to keep the guy from biting off his tongue. Before he could come up with anything, though, the need for it was over.

Timothy stopped convulsing, went rigid as a poker, then went all limp, and that was that. No need for follow-up CPR or mouth-to-mouth. There was no more prefect example of a dead man this side of Roger Kimlery.

Mrs. Potter fainted. No one paid her much mind, not even her husband who—down on bloodied and bruised knees—had problems of his own.

Someone screamed: it was Mrs. Candly, the way Dane later figured.

Mrs. Simpson's mouth was agape and only capable of making little hissing sounds.

The hotel staff, manager included, stood around wide-eyed, obviously without the foggiest notion as to what to do. Bodies, snipers, deaths, pandemonium, and hysteria, obviously weren't included in any of their areas of expertise.

* * * * * * *

CAPITÁN RODRÍGUEZ DE MANTÁÑEZ had started out from Cuzco with instructions to investigate a murder at Machu Picchu. En route, he'd been handed a message that there was now, suddenly, a sniper loose on the mountain in question, shooting at—or having shot—two U.S. tourists. Good-bye lucrative U.S. tourist dollars!

At Machu Picchu, he was immediately greeted by one dead man gone purple and sprawled upon the hotel verandah; one woman (dead?) a few feet away from the downed man; another woman wounded; another man down on his knees, wailing like a banshee. That was all before he even got his first glimpse of the bird-pecked corpse (male?) almost totally concealed beneath a rock pile off in the Inca ruins.

CHAPTER THREE

WITHIN FOUR DAYS, the soldiers found the knife, the rifle, the bottle of poison, and Timothy Jackson's knapsack, all stashed in the same spot among the ruins.

Captain Mantáñez fit all of those puzzle pieces into a solution that was satisfactory for him and, he suspected, would be equally satisfactory for his superiors: In short, madman Timothy stabbed the man in the rock pile, shot Helen, James Buchanan and poisoned himself in sick-mind remorse and/or in fear of being caught.

The soldiers, also, found Dane's SIG 49 where *he*'d hidden it, but Captain Mantáñez conveniently believed that gun was merely one Timothy had kept in reserve.

It way all too neat and tidy, but Dane certainly didn't say so. Timothy hadn't looked the killer type. This might have been the reason The Mentlic Group sent him. However, there was something about his small but admittedly wiry physique that didn't match the body-to-body contact Dane had experienced with the killer in the fog. Dane had participated in enough contact sports, and military hand-to-hands, to know Timothy hadn't been the one squeezing Dane's life away. Which meant Timothy wasn't likely to have shot at Dane and hit Helen, let alone poisoned himself in fear of detection by Captain Mantáñez's quick *let's-find-a-solution-to-this* scrutiny.

Dane wasn't about to identify the dead man in the rock pile as Roger, employee of Dayklan Incorporated, let alone explain what Dane, an employee of United Courier Service, presently assigned to Dayklan, was doing on that foggy night before, wrestling with a killer. Nor was he up to detailing why he was so sure he was the target when Helen got hers. The inspector's workable solution—right or wrong—meant the quarantine was over and lifted; Dane could finally get out with the stones Gregory so badly wanted in Cuzco.

* * * * * * *

GETTING OUT REQUIRED the ride down the mountain, and the descent was like falling from a skyscraper and, on the way down, imagining the final splat.

"Give me a break!" Dane pleaded as the van hit yet another bump on the Hiram Bingham and was —for not the first time—airborne. It landed with a jolt and continued its mad career down the mountainside.

"Can we make it?" Helen took Dane's full weight as the van whipped precariously around another hairpin turn.

Dane wasn't giving favorable odds. He assumed the driver had been paid to see they didn't make it. Life was cheap in Peru. Wages were low. A whole family could survive for a year, maybe more, on what an average American spent on one dinner in a restaurant. Say to a Peruvian peasant, *kill someone for me*. Offer him, by way of incentive, money enough to feed him and his for life. See what happened.

Dane had walked into this van-on-the-move death trap with his eyes wide open. Might as well have given him, too, a hammer and nails to secure the lid of his speeding coffin! He should have known better. He should have recognized the potential for someone ending it all for Dane this way, but he hadn't thought the enemy had access to the van. The vehicle had been within the security cordon erected by Captain Mantáñez. It had been up and down the Hiram Bingham several times without incident. Its brakes had seemed perfect. So, who snapped the brake cable? It couldn't be mere coincidence that *surely-this-is-a-malfunction* was happening now.

Helen's fingers dug into Dane's arm. "If they could duplicate this wild ride, they'd make a fortune on it at Disney World!"

Dane liked her unshakable sense of humor, even in crisis. She'd kept it through the ordeal on the mountain. She kept it now, only seconds and inches separating them from oblivion.

Dane might have been forewarned had the driver been visibly rough-and-tumble. Then, an alarm might have gone off: *Here's someone the right size for grabbing someone from behind and looping a rope around a neck.* Their driver, though, was small and skinny. He would blow away in the first big breeze. He didn't look even vaguely mean.

He looked downright friendly. He had a big, wide grin. He grinned even now. See him grin; see his gold front tooth gleam as he turns his head over his shoulder in response to Helen's latest squeal.

"Watch the bloody road!" Dane contemplated wrestling control from their kamikaze pilot. He'd crawl over Helen and over the front seat. He'd pump nonexistent brakes. Except disabling the driver just might only make things worse.

The van swept another hairpin turn. How many turns was that? There were an unlucky thirteen in total on the Hiram Bingham. Going off the highest was worse than going off the lowest, yes? If so, what consolation was that if you ended up dead, either way?

The van, seemingly reared up on two side wheels, tilted Dane over the abyss. Open the car door directly next to him, and he would tumble onto the next road meander directly below. He'd lie there, breathing his last, while the van came on down to run him over to make sure the job was well-done.

In the valley, there awaited a seemingly toy-like train. The people, boarding, or waiting to board, were more ant-like than human. There was a long way between all of that and the spot where Dane, Helen, the van, and the van's driver, barreled down the mountain.

Tires skidded and sprayed new tidal waves of gravel off the edge of the roadway. Dust spewed behind the descending vehicle like exhaust from a malfunctioning rocket.

Dane was carsick to boot: which made it all P-E-R-F-E-C-T—*NOT!*

"Can't we slow down?" It was Helen.

If Dane *could* slow them, he would. If the driver was inclined, at all, to slow them, which seemed more and more unlikely, he didn't put out the effort. They were on a one-way rollercoaster ride to oblivion.

So, what would become of the rocks in Dane's pocket? Would they melt in the resulting crash's fireball? There was *always* a fireball—in movies in the theater and on TV. Or, would a van fender disengage here, a hood separate there, a crankshaft come unglued: piecemeal disintegration? Would there be enough left of anything, or anyone, to ponder the why, what, and wherefore?

"I do believe we made it," Helen congratulated as the van squealed to a stop in the parking lot. A storm cloud of dust roared in from behind and consumed them.

"You shouldn't be allowed anywhere near the wheel of a car!" Dane bellowed at the still smiling driver. Then, he choked on the dust seeped through each and every crack and cranny.

"He doesn't speak English," Helen said. "Only *Quechua*."

Dane slid open the side door and climbed out on wobbly legs.

It was hot. It was muggy. It was dusty. Unlike on the mountain, there were no breezes in this deep-deep geographic depression to clear away natural pollutants. Dust took all day to settle. It painted everyone and everything powdery gray.

"Did you really think we were goners?" Helen insisted she be allowed to carry her own bags. Her bad arm was already out of its sling, wrapped in a *bandage-gone-from-white-to-pewter* in their hair-raising zoom down the mountain.

Let her smile and think it funny. She thought the *real* danger had ended with Timothy Jackson poisoned, but Dane knew better. Someone wasn't above tampering with brakes—no matter this apparent false alarm.

"Didn't *you* think we were done for?" he challenged her.

"Well...." Helen wiped sweat and dust from her forehead. "I do remember the ride up when my driver never did have more than two of the van wheels on the road at one and the same time."

They bought train tickets and checked their baggage, all except their carry-ons.

They found shade on the depot verandah. No sitting on a stuffy train until they had to. It was a long trip to Cuzco, all uphill; the three-and-a half hour downhill Cuzco-to-Machu-Picchu trip could, in reverse, extend to six hours, depending upon how many times the train stopped for stray animals on the grade.

"Do you know that guy, by any chance?" Helen asked.

"What guy?" Dane dislodged a gob of chewing gum from the sole of his right boot. He wished people would go back to smoking!

"Him."

Yeah, Dane knew *him*. Name: Lenard Gilly. Less than a pro, too, if Helen could spot his sorry undercover ass. What chance did Lenard have with real opposition experts in the field?

"No, why?" Dane couldn't very well admit that Lenard was another United Courier man, probably likewise attached to Dayklan Incorporated, and probably there to get the package from Dane that had already spent too much time getting this far. Well, Dane would only be too happy to turn over those three nondescript pieces of gravel in his pocket.

"He was staring, Helen said. "I thought he was actually about to come on over and say hello."

Way to go Lenard! Why not put a placard around your neck? *I'm a courier on assignment to Dayklan!*

Dane took stock of the other people. Aside from Captain Mantáñez and his soldiers, there were a few familiar faces from the hotel. However, most of the hotel guests had opted for the later, three-o'clock train. The majority of unfamiliar faces were locals, complete with chickens and piglets in wicker carry-ons. This milk-run had never been the most popular with tourists. The next swarm of which would be allowed officially in from Cuzco at seven a.m. the next morning.

A boy and his girl debated heading up the mountain, now that it was officially reopened, and they'd inadvertently ended up at the right place at the right time; there was apparently a plane connection in Lima to be weighed against this one-time, now-or-never situation. Their decision to head up the mountain eliminated them from Dane's list of suspects. He wished them luck as they began bartering for a ride up the Hiram Bingham with the *smiling kamikaze pilot* who had brought Helen and Dane on down.

Dane was interested in the muscular, redheaded loner who leaned nonchalantly against a porch support. The man had a knapsack, khaki shirt, khaki shorts. He had roughed-up hiking boots. Dane wondered what the guy, probably in his early forties, was doing seeing the country on foot when, nine times out of ten, roughing it was an indulgence only of the fancy-free and stringently-budgeted young. By middle-age, men were usually too involved with career, family, and making a living to be out trekking Peru. Granted, there were always mid-life crises to eject a few adventurous guys out of the mainstream. On the other hand, Dane couldn't be too careful.

There was a zonked-out specimen who had had one cup too many of coca tea—or whatever. He got stares from Captain Mantáñez who finally went over and asked for I.D. The kid, albeit lethargically, produced it. Apparently satisfied, Mantáñez went back to his briefly interrupted conversation with one of his men.

There was a young couple leafing through a tour book that was suspiciously too fat and heavy for *anyone* to lug around Peru.

Not everybody took advantage of the stop to stretch before departure. Some on-board passengers visibly snoozed or pretended to snooze, their heads propped against dirty widows. Some walked the aisles. Laughter hinted someone's joke. An out-of-tune guitar accompanied an out-of-tune singer, somewhere.

"I'm sorry to leave," Helen pulled back Dane's attention. "It didn't turn out too badly."

She motioned for a dirty-faced little girl who carried a tray of for-sale goodies. The youngster was a scruffy miniature of the cigarette girls in all those forties' movies. Helen selected a small triangular container of orange drink. She offered one to Dane who declined; the stuff was too cloying for his taste.

"You're right," he conceded belatedly. "It could have turned out a lot worse." For instance, he wasn't dead, like Roger; he wasn't wounded, like Helen. But would his luck run out eventually? It was, after all, a long 112 kilometers to Gregory in Cuzco.

"Still, *all* things do come to an end." She deposited her empty pop carton in a nearby cardboard box used for train-station garbage.

The train was ready to go, and stragglers began boarding.

First-class was better than Dane expected. The seats were actually padded. All the chickens and pigs rode coach. From somewhere, Lenard had summoned enough smarts not to sit in Dane's lap.

Everyone looked innocent enough, which wasn't saying they were. A couple of Peruvian businessmen in suits looked too hot as they played cards. A fat Peruvian grandmother, grandson in tow, busily cooled them both with an incongruous Japanese fan. An elderly couple, each clutching a blue travel bag with white AMERICAN EXPRESS® logo emblazoned thereon, looked as if they'd rather be somewhere—anywhere—else. An elderly man, in a Hawaiian shirt, snored none too silently. The woman across from the snorer (his wife?) knitted a sweater. No one looked anxious to take Dane on. He was definitely on a roll.

The train went through a grand mal seizure. Somewhere in second class, a chorus of young voices raised in hearty beginning of the old classic, "One Hundred Bottles of Beer on the Wall." As if that were her cue, Helen excused herself to go to the bathroom.

Dane enviously eyed the sleeping man who, undisturbed by anything, snored all the louder.

Sunshine entered through closed windows and refused to leave: the resulting heat a prime example of the greenhouse effect. The trapped warmth was narcotic. However, sleep was the last thing Dane could afford. If he were going to be taken out, he wanted to see by whom. He wanted to know when and where and how.

The woman laid down her knitting. She exercised her cramped fingers in claw-like motions. She sensed Dane watching and, before going back to working on her sweater, gave him a friendly smile. He wouldn't have been surprised to see her stand up, right then and there, and mow him down with an Uzi snatched from her knitting bag. Paranoia setting in! So much so that he awoke from an unscheduled and unwanted snooze with a jerk and a groan. His sounds drew pleasant smiles from all around.

How in the hell had he inadvertently fallen asleep?

He checked his watch. It hadn't been much of nap. Nevertheless, the singers were down to ten bottles of beer on the wall, and Helen should have been back, unless there was one very long line at the toilet.

Dane stretched and stood. He had a chance here to find Lenard and see where the jerk was holed up and trying, probably failing, to look inconspicuous. It was for Dane's best interest to know from where he might hope for backup.

The restroom in his car had no line and no Helen. Dane used it; he wasn't now, nor had he ever been, thrilled by the balancing act required: all that rocking and rolling, from side to side, simultaneous with ongoing forward momentum. There was no water with which to wash his hands or his boots; the latter pissed-splashed by the time he'd finished with the facilities.

Helen still hadn't returned to her seat, and the singers had stopped.

Dane took connecting doors into an adjoining car. Helen wasn't there, either. Neither was Lenard. There *was* a rough, wrestler-type who deserved a second look. So what if the guy was reading a comic book; you didn't need genius I.Q. to smash bones and squeeze off oxygen. So what if the sweet little old lady, sitting directly beside the brooding hulk, said, "Henry, honey, pass mother one of those chocolate biscuits." Dane was staying clear of that duo in any dark tunnels.

Mantáñez and his soldiers were grouped in the next car. They were too many eggs in the same basket for Dane's comfort. An enemy, taking out just that one car, could eliminate a lot of defensive firepower.

The soldiers didn't look as if they were expecting trouble, but why should they? Informality was the order of the hour. Shoes and uniform blouses were off. A bottle of *pisco* (it tasted like it sounded!), made the rounds; not for the first time by the sounds of things. At least one girlie magazine was getting leers. Three of the men were playing what, considering their varying stages of undress, might be strip poker. Mantáñez, fully dressed and coolly aloof, ignored it all, preferring his newspaper; he didn't even look up when Dane walked by.

Two train cars later, Dane spotted Helen standing in an aisle parenthesized by empty seats and the heavy smell of toilet disinfectant; the latter probably responsible for no passengers. He waved, and she waved back.

Still no sign of Lenard, though, and there was only the second-class cars beyond. Lenard would be of little help if too far removed.

"Hi!" Helen sounded cheerful but a bit strained. "Long time no see; or, in my case, long time no pee."

"You do know there are about six empty toilets back that way?" Dane nodded in the direction from which they'd both come. "You a masochist?"

"Don't make me laugh," she warned. She looked genuinely pained between spurts of giggles. "This has become a case of retreat now impossible in the face of high odds in favor of a probably very embarrassing accident."

"What makes you think *whomever* is going to oblige by vacating any time soon?"

"Maybe if you put in a good word?"

Dane knocked. A lady in distress was as good an excuse as any. "We have someone with a bit of a bladder problem out here." He delivered a couple more knocks, more forceful this time. "If you could see your way clear to vacate for just a few minutes, I'm sure the lady would be most appreciative."

Still getting no reply, he gave Helen a shrug.

She raised her right eyebrow in beats-me expression.

"I can't tell you how funny I'm going to find this if we've been talking to an empty toilet," Dane warned.

"Tell me about it," Helen agreed.

Dane pushed down the door handle. The latch made a sound that would have warned any unfinished occupant of ensuing intrusion.

Helen demurely put her hand over her eyes, and Dane pushed.

The door wasn't actually locked; it was blocked by something, or by somebody, inside. Dane put his shoulder to it and really gave it the old heave-ho.

"Someone deaf *and* dumb?" Helen suggested.

Dane found enough space to see inside, and the four-letter *d-word* was *dead*. Suddenly, he wanted Helen out of there long enough for him to take a closer look at Lenard who had a knife buried to its pearl-handle in his chest.

Helen didn't have to be told twice to get Captain Mantáñez; *dead-man-in-a-toilet* was as powerful an anti-diuretic as ever there was!

* * * * * * *

"TELL ME IT'S COINCIDENCE!" Helen insisted. Outside, the landscape continued to rush on by.

"What else?" Dane feigned ignorance.

"Three dead men," Helen reminded. "Two murdered. One suicide. The man in the ruins. Then, Timothy What's-his-name? Now, this guy in the toilet. One. Two. Three. How many people go through life and never stumble over even one corpse, let alone three; two of which were done in by foul play?"

"4,600,700,622 to one?" Dane ventured. "The odds, I mean."

"Funny!" Helen rewarded with an appreciative grin. "But *do* be serious. Three dead men, and you and I fired on in the ruins."

"You aren't involved in something nefarious, without telling me?" Dane was the pot calling the kettle black; the best defense was an offense. "Captain Mantáñez thinks all the deaths are drug-related." Leave it to the good captain to come up with an explanation that *could* work.

"How are they drug-related?"

"*I* haven't the foggiest," Dane confessed. "All the victims seemed to be traveling Peruvian back roads. For fun? For profit? Best to ask the Captain, not me, to share his enlightenment."

"Why those potshots taken at us?" Helen wanted to know.

"Which brings us back to coincidence," Dane said. He had answers but not for Mantáñez, and not for Helen; he felt guiltier about the latter. "We've unluckily been in the wrong places at the wrong times."

"Amen!" she sat back and closed her eyes.

"Tired?" His own sleepiness was a thing of the past.

"Exhausted! But how can I possibly let myself sleep with all of this going on?" She opened her eyes and rubbed her temples. "I can't figure that guy dead in the toilet without my having heard or seen *anything*."

"He didn't have much time to make much of a help-me fuss once the knife went in," Dane explained. His early life in the outdoors had given him a working knowledge of knives and guns that had been honed by his time spent in the military. "The murder weapon couldn't have been better placed to keep him silent. As for you seeing anything, how could you, unless you'd been in there with him?"

"With *them,*" Helen corrected. "I don't think he killed himself, do you?"

"Not too likely," Dane agreed.

"I was standing right outside the door," Helen pointed out.

"Obviously, not the whole time," Dane begged to differ.

"I should have seen the killer arrive or leave, yes?"

"What if the killer came in from second-class before you got there?" Dane ventured. "Or, what if he came in and/or left by the window?"

"Window?" Helen didn't buy that for a minute. "Without the guy inside registering some surprise at a visit from an acrobat?"

"Don't assume the killer was unexpected," Dane reasoned. "One guy might have been buying drugs, the other selling. The deal might have gone sour." That worked for Mantáñez. So what that Dane knew better?

Squealing brakes cut off conversation. A percussionistic bump, bump, bump was background accompaniment and became increasingly louder. Passengers made sounds, too. None of it, however, seemed to have any connection to Helen suddenly catapulted against Dane; both of them cascaded to the floor as the entire train car vibrated like Jell-O around them.

Dane and Helen's world turned topsy-turvy. What was ceiling and floor became walls. What were walls became ceiling and floor.

There was an exploding crack of splintering timber, bending metal, and breaking glass, as a portion of the floor-now-wall bulged beneath an exterior-delivered battering-ram force. There was more noise and more jolts, the latter less forceful as the seconds ticked on.

"Helen?" Dane asked. He was numb all over.

"What did I do to deserve this?" Her right leg was pinned under Dane's body.

Dane helped her to her feet, but only after he got her assurance she was okay.

People in other cars weren't so lucky. Mrs. Quinn, a teacher from Spokane, Washington, had a bloody nose. Mr. Juárez-Mendoza, a Lima candy salesman, had a badly cut leg. Mrs. Gooseland, a widow from Manchester, England, mumbled incoherently. Mme. Fellier, a French postmistress on holiday, was hysterical....

The train had become shattered pieces of metal vertebrae along the track. The engine was belly-up in a cloud of hot steam and turning wheels, the latter going nowhere. Passengers appeared like leaking body fluid from gaping wounds of a sliced and diced boa constrictor.

Dane pulled himself out one window and gave Helen a lift to join him outside. She was wobbly and needed him for support.

"Mr. Wilcox!" Captain Mantáñez called to Dane from the top of an upended car up the way. "Can you spare a hand over here, please?

"Helen, you'd better sit until you get back your equilibrium," Dane instructed and left her temporarily for the catwalk of mangled train parts.

Order wasn't easily brought from the chaos, but the situation benefited from an obliging Indian village, close by, whose inhabitants not only arrived in assistance but volunteered a deserted warehouse left over from a sugar-production venture gone sour three decades earlier.

Phone land-lines were mysteriously down, cell-service still nonexistent; a messenger was sent on foot to Palma to relay news of the disaster.

The shadows inside the warehouse got deeper as the afternoon progressed. The dead, dying, dead-tired, and dazed, were scattered on all sides. There wasn't much by way of supplies, but everyone held out hope that medicines and medical personnel were just on the horizon. Until that happened, there wasn't much to be done, except for the less traumatized to make their best efforts to see the less fortunate were as comfortable as possible.

Dane kept regular tabs on Helen, although usually from a distance, as he offered assistance one place and she did the same elsewhere in the dark but-hardly-cool warehouse. Once she'd taken a well-deserved break and exited the building through a rot-caused hole in the wall, but Dane's attempts to follow and join her were interrupted by a man whose badly broken leg needed a splint. By the time Dane had the man a little more comfortable, Helen was back inside.

Finally, Dane decided it was time to give himself a brief respite or drop. He was determined to coax Helen to join him. Luckily, she was more than ready and willing for another break by the time he reached her with the suggestion.

"I keep telling myself I'm not going to be of any help whatsoever, dead on my feet," she rationalized.

She got no arguments from Dane. "Smart woman!"

She led the way to the outside, via the route she'd taken earlier through nature's breach of the wall. The evidence of accompanying rot within the standing framework insinuated a building that might well collapse under its own weight, at any time; that was additional worry neither Dane nor Helen was willing to take on at the moment.

"I've wanted to get you aside, anyway," Helen admitted and continued to lead the way.

Surprisingly, outside was no less oppressing, heat-wise, except for sunlight on the wane; still no helicopter in sight or sound. Wind-blown mists already forming on a nearby mountaintop were in direct contrast to the breathlessness still cupped at the lower elevation.

"Over here," Helen instructed and proceeded to enter a patch of hot shade furnished by a copse of low-growing trees.

Dane plopped down and used one tree trunk for a back support. He patted a place beside him, disappointed when Helen didn't immediately succumb to the temptation.

"I picked up these, earlier," she said. She knelt, her back to Dane, and he couldn't see to what *these* referred.

He was still unenlightened when she got to her feet with the bundle of bloody rags and carried it over. She squatted to show him. Actually, it was only one rag: the remnants of a man's shirt that unfolded to reveal....

"The badly wounded soldiers who had these on them didn't need them by the time I got to them." Helen nodded at the revealed guns. "I knew I'd feel safer with one; and, since your *protect-us-from-the-sniper-on-the-mountain* weapon was confiscated by Mantáñez at Machu Picchu...."

"Brilliant!" Dane filled the pause with his genuine appreciation for her initiative and scrounging abilities in a crisis situation. He was more than a little embarrassed that he hadn't been as enterprising. "You know how to use these?" Both pistols were Obregon which hadn't been manufactured for some years.

"Dad had a Colt M1911A1, and he used to take me shooting. We lived in gun-filled LA, remember?"

The Obregon looked like a Colt but operated on an entirely different principle. However, none of the details about adaptation of the old Steyr-Hahn system meant that Helen's past experience wouldn't give her adequate capability for firing this gun, here and now; so, Dane stopped short of the ballistics lesson and just checked magazines for bullets. One had seven shells, one had five. He divided the ammunition evenly. He suspected he'd benefit more than Helen from a full clip, but that was only because of where he planned to go from here; it had nothing to do with her skill as a marksman. However, Helen had engineered the cache and, what with the ongoing indiscriminate killings, who knew but that she wouldn't soon find herself just as in need, as Dane, of a fully-loaded gun?

"I want you to listen to what I say very carefully." Dane wasn't sure he hadn't already wasted too much time. The survivor instinct which had told him to vacate the premises, as soon as he'd survived the train, had deserted him in the face of so many people who obviously needed help. Now, none of those people could benefit without doctor and medical supplies, and Helen's ingenuity assured him he wasn't leaving behind a woman who couldn't cope. He thanked his lucky stars that he hadn't been saddled with the archaic-stereotype weak female who fainted at the drop of a hat and turned her ankle on the first protruding tree root.

He hesitated, not because he'd reconsidered that Helen deserved a full explanation, but because he was genuinely going to miss her company in the days to come. Nevertheless, he was an albatross around her pretty neck that she definitely needed to shed.

"I work for an organization called United Courier Service," he said. "We take on assignments from companies, sometimes from governments, who want things discretely moved from one place—one city—to another."

He was glad he'd never gotten around to his *trail-guide-in-the-Washington-woods* story. This way, he came off less the liar who had to cover past prevarications.

"Sometimes the packages we care are valuable. More often, they're only of importance to the sending and receiving ends. Business papers needed for a merger. Machinery. Pieces of equipment. Replacement parts that benefit from someone along to make sure paperwork doesn't get lost in the transportation system."

"You're here, in Peru, on assignment, then?"

He told her about Dayklan, The Mentlic Group, SIS, and the SIS-designated blood-resolution minerals in Guatemala and Peru. She had the graciousness and good sense to let him finish before she made any comment.

"Let me see if I have this straight. There are satellites in orbit around the Earth that have the electronic capabilities to scan the surface of the planet. Wave-lengths reflected back to those satellites are relayed to computers at Dayklan and/or The Mentlic Group, where they're converted to curves on a graph. Also, programmed into the computers are identifying curves of all known minerals. Curves computed from the SIS scans are compared to curves on file, matched with those in-file curves, after which the individual minerals so located and matched are assigned color designates—yellow for gold, silver for silver, black for lead—on a map. Unknown minerals, not so easily matched, are temporarily assigned other designates. Like blood-red?"

Obviously, Helen didn't need things explained more than once. Dane tried to remember if he'd been nearly as cognizant of how things worked when he'd received his initial briefing. If not, he preferred to blame the Dayklan man who'd been far less succinct and concise with his facts than Dane, with Helen, had been.

"Blood-red resolution, here," Helen continued, "refers to two deposits of the same unidentified

mineral, with locations in Guatemala and Peru. The
Mentlic Group, whose SIS beat Dayklan's into the
sky overhead, has sewed up both deposit sites and
refuses Dayklan access. Curious, Dayklan sent a geologist to scout the ore deposit here in Peru. That
geologist—"

"Roger Limlery."

"—became the first man dead on the mountain."

Dane nodded affirmation. No need confusing
things by any mention of the disappeared Jim
Chimchuck who'd been sent along as Roger's baby-
sitter.

"Roger killed, presumably by someone from
The Mentlic Group, but not before he passed on to
you the samples he'd gathered on the Peruvian site.
All the rest of this—the death of Terry What's-his-
name, someone shooting at us, the dead man on the
train, the train crash—has to do with The Mentlic
Group's ongoing efforts to keep samples from
Dayklan."

"Keep *these* from Dayklan." Dane rolled the un-
impressive rocks within the fingers and palm of one
hand.

"Potential ingredients for some new and deadly
bomb?"

"Nothing so ominous; at least, rumor says so.
We're more likely talking a possible major breakthrough in superconductivity." He would have left it
at that, with an attending comment that there was no
sense boring her with technical gobbledygook, but
he thought that would probably come off patronizing. "Electricity made at one spot has to be trans-
ported to some other spot along a metal conductor
that presently offers, depending upon what it's made

of, varying degrees of resistance; i.e. power sent doesn't equal wattage delivered."

She didn't look confused and proved she'd likely seen the PBS television documentary that provided far more detail than Dane offered. "Super-conductors designed to make final output more fully equal that of initial input?"

"Exactly."

"And with increasing demands on existing power sources, and the reluctance of some nations, the U.S. included, to convert to either nuclear facili-ties, or some other alternative source or sources of energy, maximization of existing electricity be-comes big business."

"With big profits."

"Enough to kill for." It wasn't a question

Dane answered anyway: "I'm afraid so."

"None of which gave your employer a clue that it might have been better to send in an army instead of a few good men?"

"One international conglomerate doesn't ever initiate an all-out war with another, unless it's cer-tain beforehand that the profits to be gained will ex-ceed the enduring animosities and complications that can result. Beside that, the army you suggested would cost a great deal of money at a point where Dayklan can't be certain its scientists will be able to exploit the mineral to the extent The Mentlic Group so obviously believes its own scientists can. It's not as if the ability of one scientist, on one side, is iden-tical to the ability of another scientist, on the other side. Granted, The Mentlic Group seems to think Dayklan does have that capability, but the Dayklan money-men remain reluctant to commit the funds needed for any massive assault; not without some idea of the potential for profits that they figure can be computed through analysis of a small sample. Also, an army would alert the Peruvian government to the possible value: a disadvantage to any company if and when it begins bargaining for mineral rights."

"Isn't that last a superfluous precaution, taken by Dayklan, when it's so likely The Mentlic Group will be in there jacking up the ante in any bidding war?"

"It's the Mentlic Group's cross to bear that of all places this second deposit could be, it turns up in Peru. The Group hasn't had official entrée to this country since Dayklan took over all the copper, gold, lead, zinc, and iron concessions from it in the seventies, after The Group did some fancy double-book accounting that cheated Peru out of millions. All The Group is doing here, now, is pursuing a delaying action, presumably of long enough duration, for them to sew up valuable patents as regards potential uses of the new metal."

"You don't think the Peruvian government is going to look unkindly on all of these corporate shenanigans if and when it finds out all these deaths were caused by Dayklan and The Mentlic Group more interested in maximizing profits, down the road, than in immediately letting Peru know the potential in its own backyard?"

Dane shrugged. "It's definitely a bargaining chip the Peruvian's might have in their corner, during negotiations. But what do I know, in the interim? I'm just one very low man on the totem pole."

"I'd say events have some people, me included, thinking you're a bit more than that."

"As good a reason as any for me to say good-bye."

He was glad, but admittedly just as disappointed, when Helen didn't put up any argument to his leaving.

"As I'm obviously a target," he continued, "I'm better off separated from innocents, like you, who might end up dead by mere association." He slipped the rocks back into his pocket.

"Well!" Still squatted, Helen crab-walked to his tree trunk. "I admit you turned out to be a bit more than I bargained for when I first decided to treat myself to a Peruvian holiday."

"Maybe when this is all over...."

He felt vulnerable in the pause. No amount of years made him immune to a put-down.

"Call me if you're ever in Los Angeles," she said.

He breathed an inward sigh of relief and felt in surprisingly good humor. "I hope you don't mind my taking one of these guns with me."

"I think you'd do better to take both of them," she offered in alternative. "I'll be safe enough once you've flown the coop."

The lady's reasoning was impeccable. He really wished....

"One more thing you can take with you." She gave him a warm kiss on the cheek that conjured pleasurable gooseflesh along his arms, despite the continuing high degree of heat generated by the dying day.

However, that combination of inner and outer stimulation was paled by the sudden eruption of the warehouse into a voluminous ball of orange-red flame.

The flash was blinding. The heat of it singed Dane and Helen's hair and provided the attending recognizable stench. The shock wave slammed them against the tree which bent, along with other nearby trees, then snapped with an attending barrage of splinters.

Where there had been a building and people, there was now only crackling flame and inky smoke.

A piece of airborne white-hot corrugated roofing branded its noisy descent through hot air and heat-wilted leaves with a loud THWUMP! of collision with the charred earth not more than six feet from where Dane and Helen were helplessly sprawled.

CHAPTER FOUR

DANE'S EARS RANG; he had a nosebleed. He staunched the latter with a quick wipe from one smoldering sleeve. It took several blinks and swallows to lubricate his eyes and his throat sufficiently to see and swallow properly. His legs were rubbery when he tried to put his weight on them; he had to be satisfied with a slow crawl to Helen's side.

A large wooden splinter, propelled from the blast-shattered tree, was crocheted into the cloth of Helen's blouse and gave Dane pause. Only the absence of accompanying blood on the punctured material relaxed him for his closer look that assured him that her flesh, directly underneath, was miraculously spared any penetration.

Further encouragement came when Helen groaned and actually managed, with his assistance, a sitting position.

"What...?" Her question didn't need any more elucidation than that.

By the time Dane got around to, "Someone blew the warehouse," Helen could see that for herself. She didn't need elaboration, either, as to whom that *someone* probably was.

"They're mad!" Helen's judgment echoed Dane's own.

Good Samaritans from the nearby village were again on the scene, mainly in silhouette as they poured buckets of water on a fire obviously not about to be quenched until the last of the building was consumed.

"I've got to move out of here." Dane's statement was as much an incentive for him to get up and go, as it was his final good-bye to Helen.

"*We* have to get out of here," she amended. "If The Mentlic Group got close enough to blow the warehouse, they got close enough to see something definitely going on between you and me. Or, do you disagree that our relationship has progressed beyond two people teaming up for a few moments of shared good times in Peru?"

Whether they were on the verge of any kind of romantic involvement, Dane couldn't deny that Helen's association with him had made her especially vulnerable. Were the bad guys to assume Helen of any importance to Dane, they'd have no qualms making her a pawn to be used, however violently, to get to him. The closer an eye Dane kept on Helen, the better he'd be able to keep her and him from any such fate.

Except—"I'm not exactly the safest person to be with at the moment."

"Tell me about it. However, I don't prefer the alternative of sticking around here to see your opposition at closer range."

"Firstly, let's see if either of us is up to walking." He made it to his feet, wobbled momentarily, then adjusted for reasonable balance. So far, so good. "Up we come." He hooked his hands with hers.

She came to her feet with only the slightest bobble. She shifted tentatively from one foot to the other to assure she would remain standing once he let go. "Nothing *seems* broken." She brushed off her arms and legs in search for damage visible but not felt. She removed the wood splinter which, as jewelry, was far too macabre for her taste.

Meanwhile, Dane decided that, once again, he'd come out of near disaster pretty much intact; knock on wood. He retrieved their two pistols from where events had repositioned them. Both weapons were dusty but seemed as ready to fire-as they could be, short of pulling their triggers and attracting undue attention.

"I say: down the valley far enough to assure concealment of our departure from the immediate area, and then veer toward the escarpment and the old Inca Road." It was Dane's suggestion, surprisingly voiced by Helen. She smiled at his expression, obviously pleased that her mind hadn't short-circuited on events to where she couldn't reason the obvious. "The first place The Mentlic Group is going to check for us is wherever rescue or work parties come within hailing distance. Our best bet is to make it to the nearest town on foot, where we'll more easily blend into the crowd."

He wasn't about to disagree.

Without further ado, they started out. If each had second thoughts about not sticking around to give succor to their fellow survivors, those were overruled by shared rationalization that Dane and his cargo could best protect all innocents by steering clear of them.

They would have made better time had they walked the railway, because the valley was otherwise cluttered with tropical vegetation through which they had to weave. However, walking the tracks was out of the question, because rescue teams, hopefully already on the way, would access the wreckage that way, or by the faster air corridors directly overhead; Dane and Helen had agreed that their rescue, those ways, wasn't necessarily to their advantage when other than just well-intentioned people were on the prowl for survivors.

They stocked up on bananas, by way of food supply, and then turned toward the steeper incline that would eventually shed all vegetation. If it looked as if they were headed for unfriendly terrain, that was only half right. The ancients hadn't descended into the valley except to plant and harvest crops; their cities had commanded mountain sites, and the connecting roadways ran mountain spines, not directly alongside rivers too wild for navigation by dugouts.

"Picoguau strike you as our best bet?" Helen munched a banana definitely starchier than its counterparts in U.S. supermarkets.

"And a quick bus out of there to Cuzco," Dane agreed. "After I call ahead and tell my people to expect us."

"Want to estimate our travel time?"

In unison, they maneuvered for better concealment amidst vegetation as a helicopter passed overhead, and off to one side.

"A couple of days to Picoguau, not accounting for unforeseen complications," Dane returned to Helen's question. "From Picoguau to Cuzco depends on how often the buses run, and if the bus we get is in better condition than the majority." He didn't continue. He was well aware of the obstacles still ahead of them, and so was Helen.

Helen gave her banana peel flight, assured of its biodegradability upon landing. She wasn't pleased by the way her leg muscles were already starting to bunch into impossibly tight knots. Hopefully, they'd loosen before she began any serious climbing.

They might have covered more distance before night, but they opted for the convenience of another banana grove. By then, they'd headed far enough up the valley wall so that fruit was scarcer. Besides, there was something enticing about leaves that might be stripped for use as blankets.

They settled in for a night that wasn't restful, despite their exhaustion. It was hard to feel safe in a world where the enemy, a deadly one at that, appeared with such disastrous regularity; apprehension wasn't conducive to the unconsciousness of good sleep. Every sound, and the night was full of them, hinted repercussions more life-threatening than they turned out to be.

"Only some scurrying rodent." Dane's assurance dispelled his own anxiety, as well as Helen's, at the latest sound.

"Why does the thought of rats on the prowl do absolutely nothing to reassure me?" Helen pulled banana leaves over her head and fantasized silken sheets and down-stuffed pillows to lie on.

Fog, a product of the collision of rising warmer valley air with cascading cooler mountain air, was less a problem where they were than at higher altitudes, but there was enough of it to add a clammy dampness and chill that made banana leaves insufficient insulation. Dane and Helen's early-morning departure was as much a case of *chill-to-the-bones* as a need to get up and get moving.

Dane was stiff beyond belief, kept from complaining by Helen's silence in circumstances she couldn't find any easier than he did.

They heard more helicopters as the morning progressed, but their ascent kept pace with dissolving fog to the point where any sighting of them from above remained impaired.

"A train?" Helen stopped and listened.

Dane agreed. "Probably more medical supplies and work teams to clear the tracks."

Neither suggested they change their course and attempt connecting with helicopters or train. Obscurity continued to be what they wanted most, not the attending *look-at-us* notoriety their unexpected emergence would cause this far from the crash scene.

There was no mistaking their continuing determination when they finally reached the old Inca Road, a narrow pathway between two drops, one east and one west.

"My aerobics instructor would be impressed." Helen looked back and down over the distance covered. She tried to pinpoint the wreckage, but the twists and turns of the rugged terrain obliterated any real evidence of it, except for a curling of smoke which might, or might not, signify all that remained of the brutalized warehouse.

"Never mind your aerobics instructor; *I'm* impressed," Dane congratulated. Their ascent had been more of a chore than he'd anticipated. Obviously, he wasn't in as good a shape as he would have liked. He resolved to budget more gym time if and when he returned to a more humdrum existence.

A look toward Picoguau showed nothing, either. All signs of civilization were those of the long-disappeared Inca.

"Onward, is it?" Dane suggested.

"Don't put off until tomorrow…and all of that good stuff," Helen said. "At least we can be pleased that our route has substantially leveled off."

For the most, that ended all small talk while they concentrated time and energy to placing one foot in front of the other. Short breaks were equally silent as they recovered normal breathing patterns still easily thrown out of kilter by the high altitude.

That night proved more uncomfortable than the one that preceded. The fog was thicker here and arrived sooner. There were no banana tree leaves with which to cover at an elevation too cold at night, and too starved of CO_2 night or day to support greenery.

If Dane had had a bad heart, his rude awakening the next morning would have been his last. Luckily, his heart was in good condition. It survived the firing of Helen's Obregon; that didn't mean it didn't speed up as result of the massive dose of adrenaline suddenly set loose inside him.

Automatically, he rolled into a tight ball and positioned himself closer against the adjacent Inca wall; he reached for his gun, pleased to find it.

"Helen?"

She was a couple of feet away, flush against the same stone wall. Her eyes were wide. "He has a gun."

"Who?" Dane checked where her pistol was aimed but saw only stones.

"I think it's that redheaded guy from the train: the good-looking, butch number all done out in khaki."

Dane remembered the traveler too long-in-the-tooth to be thumbing his way through South America.

"Wait here!" Dane kept low in a circuitous route of reconnaissance.

He wasn't pleased by this latest development, because he'd hoped Helen and he had been assumed blown with the warehouse. Apparently, though, the enemy had more smarts than Dane had been prepared to give him.

Dane hoped to find their assailant dead or wounded by Helen's fired bullet, but the redhead, dead or not, wounded or not, apparently had had the wherewithal for retreat into the hodgepodge of ruins along the trail. If the guy were even now squirreled away in there, belly-down, lining up Dane in the sights of a rifle, he wasn't likely to be easily flushed out.

Dane returned to Helen and dropped beside her with a hug in greeting. She'd held up well, and he didn't want her falling apart at this late date. "You seem to have scared him off. He'll have second thoughts about coming back for seconds." They should be so lucky! "If we slip away now, it might take him awhile to get up the guts to come out of hiding. By then, we may have the advantage of a head start all of the way to Cuzco."

* * * * * * *

THEY ENCOUNTERED DAROLD WESLEY at noon. They rounded a bend in the trail, and there he was, leaned against a rock as he tried to puff life into a pipe that refused resurrection at that altitude.

Although he looked harmless, their first impulse was to turn tail and run. Their second, and prevailing, was to stay calm and play it by ear.

"Yo, but you scared me!" he said and *looked* surprised, too. Also, he looked exactly what he said he was: "A history student from U.C.L.A. Here to indulge my life-long passion for amateur archaeology."

Dane and Helen's story wasn't so logical, because they remained determined to keep it separate from the happenings in the valley. They saw no reason to give Darold anything he could pass on, no matter how unwittingly or unwillingly, to make any curious inquirer wonder if the two Americans he'd encountered were ones who *should* have been killed in the warehouse.

He listened sympathetically to their tale, concocted on the spot, of how their knapsacks had perversely toppled into a gorge when a piece of embankment gave way.

"Rotten luck!" He sounded appropriately sympathetic and ready with a bit of good cheer. "Luckily, you're only a few miles out of Picoguau. In the meantime, I'll treat you to a decent meal of *packaged-and-only-needing-water* stew. What do you say? I can, also, spare some raisins and walnuts to get you through tomorrow."

Darold's offer of a hot meal would have definitely been refused had there been any sign, whatsoever, of continued pursuit by the redhead. Possibly lulled into a false sense of security, Dane nevertheless found the idea of an energy-producing hot meal more inviting than he knew he should have.

"Did you make it as far as Machu Picchu?" Darold asked as he busily set up his camp stove that operated on white gas, or on kerosene, or on alcohol; or, in a pinch, even on the local rot-gut liquor.

"We were told the ruins were closed," Dane parried. "Something about a shooting."

"It's been open a couple of days now." Darold untelescoped a cooking pot and filled it with water from his canteen. "Except the only way to get there is by foot, since a nasty train wreck closed the tracks through the valley. The crash is all the talk in Picoguau at the moment."

By the time the stew was ready, Helen was almost comatose over its delicious smells. Her first spoonful was followed by compliments to the cook usually reserved for the likes of a gourmet chef. Dane's gastronomical sound effects were no less demonstrative.

Darold's mistake was in not dosing his dinner guests with a larger amount of sedative. Or, maybe, Dane's digestive tract merely responded less slowly than the average. Whatever, Dane realized what was happening before he was completely incapacitated by the narcotic.

It was a definite slowing of his motor skills that gave him his first clue; it took an inordinately long time for his spoon to travel the distance from his plate to his mouth. There was something decidedly suspicious, too, about Darold ignoring the way Helen's spoon went teeter-totter in her fingers and dropped from her hand; Helen sat with no apparent realization that her eating utensil had deserted her.

Dane took advantage of the grace period with a slow-motion action that seemed impaired to the point where Darold would certainly stop it. He pulled his gun, his fingers already too numb to pull the trigger, and he backhanded the smug Darold with the black metal.

Darold's misplaced overconfidence was paid for by his going down and out beneath the force of the blow.

Helen's lack of comment on Dane's successful cold-cocking of their host told just how far gone she was. Pulling her to her feet was like dislodging a tree from a plot of ground to which it had been securely rooted for at least the last hundred years. En route to her standing, she jettisoned her plate which followed her spoon into the dust at her feet. She wasn't steady, but neither was Dane.

"Helen, we've got to move!" Dane's ongoing battle with the drug was one he'd eventually lose, and he had two very important objectives before that happened: one, Helen and he had to find some hole into which they could crawl to hide from a revived Darold, or whomever; two, Dane had to hide the prize everyone was so hot to have from him.

He managed the latter a few yards up the trail. All three rocks conveniently slid beneath a lean-to provided by a piece of Inca masonry toppled against a more long-lasting segment of Inca wall.

Hiding Helen and him was more difficult, because not only did any lean-to they'd require have to be a large one, but it had to be situated so as to avoid any hostile search party. The farther away from Darold the better, but that was easier said than done. Helen's steps were taken only because Dane's jerks on her arm caused her reflexively to adjust her loss of balance by putting one foot in front of the other. Even that automatic remnant of coordination showed signs of rapid deterioration.

Nor was Dane's stumbling anything about which he could brag. His vision wasn't focused, either, and it performed visual tricks that constantly shifted perspective from far away to high-powered magnification.

When the ground gave way beneath him, he had sense enough to turn loose of Helen so she wouldn't take the fall with him. This left him with a genuine sense of satisfaction until it took way too long for him to hit ground. When he did hit, the jolt took his breath way, and he become one with a small avalanche of dust, rock, and loose dirt.

Unconsciousness came and went in a shorter time than he thought; anyway, its exit was accompanied by daylight hopefully the same as before he'd left it.

"Lucky me!" Dane's mumble was undecipherable by anyone without prior knowledge of what he'd said.

He began a systematic, mental check of his faculties to ascertain whether they well-functioned.

He was pleased with his aches and pains, in that their discomfort hinted of his nervous system still operational. Of course, there was a fine line between welcomed pain and pain in the extreme; paranoid, he awaited the latter.

"Helen? Helen?"

He remembered he'd left her up top, reassured once a scan of his immediate area told him she hadn't toppled down the mountain with him.

It was still a long way to the valley floor: a distance he would easily travel if he slid three yards farther and over the drop off that awaited him there.

The slope between him and the top was an obstacle course easier taken from the opposite direction. He was surprised he hadn't broken his neck, and he checked one more time to make sure shock hadn't masked any real bodily damage. Reassured, he commenced his climb. He no longer called out to Helen, not because his concern for her had lessened, but because he didn't want the enemy to hear that he was on his way to help her.

His wasn't an uninterrupted scamper, because it was decidedly rough going, and he still lacked any return to adequate coordination. Once, overly confident, he almost fell backwards. As a result, he downgraded his efforts and took more frequent rest stops. "Haste makes waste," he reasoned aloud.

Luckily, he regained the trail before sundown flooded the area with darkness and fog.

No sign of Helen, though, and there should have been if she'd remained where he'd left her.

He backtracked to where they'd succumbed to the temptation of Darold's deceptive hospitality. The only remaining evidence of previous occupancy, there, was Helen's discarded pistol with a tube of notebook paper stuffed in its barrel. Unrolled, the paper provided a series of numbers in bold, black ink: a telephone number with Cuzco exchange. Accompanying, in a decidedly masculine script, was a short note: *You should call if you ever want to see Helen alive again.*

Dane pivoted in a slow *three-hundred-and-sixty degree* turn to make another check for the enemy, and he received a slap of cold fog as it rolled up and over the edge of the escarpment. He headed for the hiding spot where he'd left the rocks, apprehensive that he might not remember where it was. Right spot or not, would the stones be there?

"Ah, yes!" His relief was as audible as his breath was suddenly visible within the increasingly chilly air.

He pocketed the stones, but he was kept from any immediate beeline to Picoguau by common-sense logic that reasoned his condition and that of the rugged terrain, combined with the fog after nightfall, might well be the death of him if he challenged all of them stacked against him.

He found a niche where he could burrow until morning, but it wasn't an easy wait. The chill brought out his every ache and pain and magnified them. He worried more and more about Helen and how long her captor would wait for Dane to call. If Dane would have died in his fall down the mountain, would Helen have thought he'd deserted her? Would frustrated lackeys of The Mentlic Group have taken Dane's no-show out on their helpless hapless victim?

He wanted to leave at first light but prudently waited until the mists lifted sufficiently for him to better judge solid rock from illusion. Helen's survival counted on him getting off this mountain alive.

People who killed so easily would have no qualms about eliminating one more woman if Dane never showed with her purchase price.

It was slow going, made slower by Dane's stiffness from his fall and from the night cold which had elaborated every affliction. His muscles needed large knots worked out, and that didn't happen until well into morning.

* * * * * * *

HE DIALED CUZCO from a land phone at the Picoguau bus station; cell service still nonexistent.

"Mr. Wilcox?" a male voice answered after two rings.

"You were expecting someone else?" Dane tried to conceal his ill temper with sarcasm.

"Mr. Wilcox?" the man repeated.

"And you're a recording?" Dane remained uncooperative.

"Mr. Wilcox?" the man was undaunted.

"Yes," Dane conceded finally; otherwise, their little song and dance could go on into the night.

"Ah, and how pleased I am to have you call." He *did* sound pleased. "This is in reference to your curiosity as to the present whereabouts of Miss Mallory, is it?"

"If you've harmed a hair on her head, I'll...." Dane left it at that. He was at a loss as to what he could actually do above and beyond what he was doing.

"She's well," the man assured. "Her momentary drug problem has resolved itself. Yours too, I trust?"

Dane was encouraged.

"Are you there, Mr. Wilcox?" Did the guy think Dane had dropped off the edge of the world, or what? Maybe he should be told just how close Dane had come to doing just that. "We don't have much time."

"Time for what?" Silly question! Dane was well aware of his situation, and he didn't like it.

"There's a bus about to leave there for Cuzco. You're not far from the bus station, are you, Mr. Wilcox?"

Dane was tempted to lie. He needed time to maneuver. He could do that by making this guy think he had to take a later bus. Once in Cuzco, he could enlist Gregory's help in putting an address to the phone number.

"Actually, we *know* exactly where you are," the man interrupted Dane's runaway thoughts. "An associate is even now watching."

Dane checked but could see no one seemingly paying him any mind.

"Board the bus for Cuzco, Mr. Wilcox," Dane was instructed. "At Quansezuan, you should somehow arrange to have the seat next to yours empty, so our representative can join you. Since *you* know what *we* want, and *we* know what *you* want, it merely comes down to the question of whether or not we can arrange the exchange before Miss Mallory experiences any permanent damage."

The line went dead.

* * * * * * *

IN QUANSEZUAN, DANE was joined by the redhead, same khaki shorts and khaki shirt, same scuffed hiking books, same knapsack. The guy's smile was deceptively charming and bemused. "Nice of you to save me a seat, old boy."

"Where's Helen?" Dane had made a muff of a blanket bought last-minute in Picoguau. The blanket wrapped Dane's hand and his gun.

"I suppose you'll shoot me if I don't tell?" The redhead didn't sound particularly threatened or concerned.

"Don't tempt me," Dane warned.

"Hey, I'm just a messenger, here," the redhead reminded. "A peon, like you."

"You were telling me about Helen," Dane prodded.

"The way I hear it, *you* know her far more intimately than I ever could."

Somehow, Dane didn't like the sound of that. "I'd watch my mouth, if I were you."

"Very well." The redhead slouched in his seat and folded his arms over his well-developed chest. He shut his eyes. "I'll try not to disturb you any longer. Wake me when we get to Cuzco, will you?" He opened his eyes and turned in Dane's direction. "Unless you drop that smart-aleck attitude of yours and decide you're interested in hearing what I have to say now."

"I'm interested only in where you have Helen."

"I'm afraid I don't know where she is."

"What's that mean?" Dane wanted an answer, and he wanted it fast.

"My employer figured you'd threaten me at gunpoint, and he didn't want me to get all blabbermouth at the thought of passing into the Great Beyond, so he made it a point *not* to tell me much. I'm instructed only *to ask* if you have the stones with you."

"You think I'm that much of a fool?" Dane bluffed. He'd had no time to put the stones anywhere safe, not when he didn't know when they'd be demanded of him for Helen's ransom. "I've made arrangements for them to reach Dayklan without me if something happens to me, or to Helen, along the way," he lied.

"We thought you might, Dane. I suppose it's okay for me to call you Dane, right? You can call me *Red*."

"I've a few choicer names I'd rather call you."

"Now, now. Name-calling is so juvenile. You must try to remember that your side lifted the stones from us in the first place. My side merely wants back what's ours by right of first-discovery."

"It was my understanding that the goods in question, the truth be known, belong to the Peruvian government."

"Finders, keepers," Red begged to differ.

"Losers, weepers," Dane thought *that* put things in even better perspective.

"*Losing* something is one thing," Red reminded. "Having it *stolen* is quite something else again."

"I'm merely a courier, try to remember," Dane reminded. That little detail seemed to have become lost in the shuffle. "I'm just trying to do my job, here."

"And I'm trying just to do *my* job, frustrated that, up until now, you've somehow managed your job far better than I've managed mine."

"Purely by luck." Dane wished he could claim more credit.

"Don't be so modest. Doing so denigrates my efforts. Besides, we make our own luck, don't we?"

"You want the stones for the safe return to me of Helen."

"Bingo!" Red confirmed. "It's settled, then, is it?"

"Not likely!"

"Oh? We're not going to haggle, are we? Surely, Helen's life isn't shoddy merchandise to be bartered over in a Cuzco bazaar."

"Such a trade-off needs approval from a higher level than me."

"You and I know it won't get approval from a higher level. Who is Helen to your bosses? They can't see her as more valuable than what we're expecting you to give up for her."

"You expect me to make this decision on my own?"

"You're a big boy, more than capable of making decisions in the field without checking in with mommy or daddy on the home front. Just take a little time to see if Helen's life doesn't compute more to you than it's likely to compute to your superiors."

"My employers won't react favorably to my fraternization with the enemy."

"Anyone who wiggled through the traps I set for you can surely outwit the amateurs on your side."

"I may have used up all my luck."

"That would be a shame. It would suddenly make my cutting up of Helen, for mailing to you a small piece at a time, my lot in life."

"You fucking perverted shit!" Dane's response drew attention and frowns from all around.

"Deteriorated to name-calling, has it?" Red said with a sigh. "All I'm trying to tell you, Dane, is how things are. My side is frustrated in having, so far, been turned back at every turn. We're used to coming out on the winning side without nearly as much effort as we've expended."

"Killing Helen isn't going to accomplish anything."

"There's something to be said for sweet vengeance, yes?" Red disagreed.

"So, just let me take this exchange proposal to my people in Cuzco."

"We've already agreed they won't go for it." Red rested his head against the back of his seat and closed his eyes. "By *we*, I'm referring to you, to me, *and* to the people who've sent me."

They rode in silence for a full fifteen minutes of bumpy roadway. The other passengers were less silent, including the piglet of one indigenous Indian lady. An obnoxious kid, age six or so, pulled the hair of his even younger sister; in turn, the sister slapped the kid hard across the top of his head.

"We'll give you until Cuzco, maybe even a tad longer, to make your decision," Red surprised as the bus slowed to maneuver a narrow stretch of road, all that was left after a recent rainfall. "I suggest you spend most of that time running through any scenario that has you approaching your boss, Gregory Smant, with the proposition that he surrender what you've brought him in exchange for an American woman he doesn't know from beans."

Despite all of Dane's efforts to believe that Gregory *would,* if put to the test, chose Helen over the three stones, his mental run-throughs just never seemed to come out that way. To Gregory, Helen was just a name with no face; a woman with whom he shared no memories.

The bus slowed for Cantalaba. Red stretched, stood, and retrieved his knapsack from where he'd stashed it in the rack above his seat.

"You're getting off?" Dane had expected the man's company right on through to the end of the line.

"I've said all I have to say. Riding bumpy Peruvian back roads with you is hardly the way I best enjoy spending my day. I do have other things to do, you know?"

Dane couldn't imagine what *other things*, considering all that came before.

"Someone will contact you in Cuzco, Dane, to finalize arrangements for the exchange. You and I know that Helen turned over for those rocks is the only humane way to go, on this, don't we?"

"And if I decide to hold you at gunpoint in exchange for Helen?" He pulled back a corner of the blanket in his lap to expose his gun for the first time.

"You and I know that I'm considered expendable," Red chided and headed down the aisle behind the woman whose piglet's high-pitched squeals insinuated no greater pleasure in having reached its destination than it had in its ride to get there.

Before the bus pulled into Puella, at each and every stop, Dane checked for, and failed to find, a cell-phone connection. Likewise, he contemplated finding and using a telephone land-line. He kept telling himself that Gregory had all the resources of Dayklan at his disposable to get Helen back. Except, all Dayklan's resources seemed more inflexibly geared toward getting the stones. As much as Dane might argue in favor of Helen's safety with Gregory, Gregory might well opt, instead, for possession of three, small, inanimate pieces of rock chipped from some blood-resolution matrix in deep Peru.

By the time the bus reached the suburbs of Cuzco, Dane was no closer to a decision. He needed far more time than he suspected anyone, Helen included, was prepared to give him.

When he walked out of the depot, he was followed by a beefy local in T-shirt and faded jeans. His *tail* looked thirty-something but could have been older or younger behind the large cigar and cigar smoke that concealed most of his face. Either the guy wasn't very good at shadowing, or it didn't much matter if Dane spotted him or not. After all, how was The Mentlic Group supposed to contact Dane for final arrangements if he faded too completely into the maze of Cuzco streets?

All the while thinking of Helen, Dane didn't exercise any of his extensive repertoire of tactics specifically designed to extract him from unwanted company. He moved from one spot to another slowly enough so that even a novice could keep tabs of where he was and what he was up to.

His clothes had become downright ratty since Machu Picchu. He bought a pair of pre-shrunk Levi's—found even in Peru. He supplemented those with a dark blue wool shirt and green jacket whose pockets were big enough and deep enough to swallow the stones without appearing distorted.

He checked into the Hotel Savoy, an ugly edifice with two advantages over the Hotel Libertador where he'd stayed before. There wasn't anyone on staff to remember that Dane had been through Cuzco en route to Machu Picchu. It had rooms with private baths; in Dane's present state of mental and physical deterioration, a hot shower more and more took on the fabled enticement of a rejuvenating fountain of youth.

He had no problems at the front desk, despite his rumpled, unclean appearance and *yes-Dane-you-do-indeed-stink* smell; he took the precaution of prominently displaying his newly purchased clothes on the countertop, with accompanying comments on how he'd just spent the last few days *enjoying Peruvian back trails*.

The shower in his room provided a miracle of hot water that stayed hot from start to finish; if it didn't conjure any immediate solutions to his problems, it did make him feel as if he could come up with something if he just put his mind to it.

Unfortunately, his shower-time was the only time he got, because his boss, Gregory Smant, waited, Browning HP35 pistol in hand, as the travel-weary, lone-towel-wrapped Dane emerged from the bathroom and headed for the new clothes laid out on the hotel bed.

Dane would have been less surprised to see Red, or Darold *of-the-drugged-stew*. After all, he'd assumed all along that his tail, the one he'd taken such pains *not* to lose, had belonged to The Mentlic Group; possibly, he'd been mistaken.

"You can't believe how relieved we were to hear that our man had spotted you in-coming at the Cuzco bus depot." Gregory's gun motioned Dane farther from the bed and into a more exposed portion of the room. "Naturally, we worked under the assumption that you were clever enough and resourceful enough to emerge with the prize, but even we were appalled by the volatility of the booby traps set for you along the way."

"Do you think we could postpone this long enough for me to put on some clothes?"

"I think we'll hold off on your dressing." Gregory sat back and crossed thin legs that were parts of his scarecrow body. He leaned his glossily oiled hair against the back of his chair, his *black-as-his-hair* eyes vacant insofar as any insights into the emotions inside him. Dane saw no friendliness in the expression that pinched the corners of Gregory's painfully thin mouth.

"Really, Gregory, I do think...."

"Let me tell you what *I* think," Gregory interrupted. "*I* think as a result of a certain interrogation course I once took, courtesy of the U.S. military establishment, that there's a certain advantage to the questioner when the questioned is partially or fully unclothed."

"This is to be some kind of confrontation, then?" It was a superfluous question, and Dane knew it. Friends didn't meet up at gunpoint.

"Our pleasure in discovering you safe and sound soon deteriorated into confusion when our phone never rang, long after we expected you to call—long after you *should have* checked in. You see, Dane, there were rumors, all along, that you had become involved with some American woman at Machu Picchu who has since turned up missing. Would you care to shed any light on that particular subject?"

"Helen Mallory."

"Right! By chance, is Helen now hanging back, embarrassed to emerge from your bathroom after your shared shower?"

"You know she's not."

"We know an awfully lot without knowing nearly enough. Now that we have you, we expect answers to all sorts of questions, and this gun is our assurance we'll get them."

"I might have expected strong-arm tactics from The Mentlic Group, but from my own side?" There was no doubt he felt more and more vulnerable as the minutes ticked by; the last of the shower water coolly evaporated from his exposed body.

"We at Dayklan pride ourselves on not being as barbaric as The Mentlic Group, but there are times that *do* require extraordinary measures. Do you know how many bodies, mainly innocents, The Mentlic Group as left scattered over the Peruvian countryside, one of whom was your fellow courier knifed on that train? We're protective of our own, Dane. We would have been equally distraught had *you* been so martyred in the line of duty. There is, however, quite another reaction toward someone who turns against us when we've done our very best by him. And there are admittedly certain of my peers, whose duties include the analysis of facts, figures, rumors, gossip, and conjecture, who have reached the tentative conclusion that you're no longer with us. Would you care to comment upon that innuendo? Unlike The Mentlic Group, we at

Dayklan aim to be fair. There's no way we jump to foregone conclusions without hearing the accused's side of the story."

"They have Helen, and they've threatened to kill her." That was the story in a nutshell; well, at least it was half of it.

"Unless *you* turn over *to them* the mineral samples," Gregory filled in for him.

"Yes."

"Which you haven't yet done? Or have you?"

"No."

"Very good." There was the slightest relaxing of tension lines around Gregory's pursed lips. "While we can very well understand your concern over the abduction of this woman, our forgiveness would be another matter should you have taken your concern for her beyond acceptable limits."

"They'll kill her, Gregory. Just like they killed at Machu Picchu, on the train, at the warehouse."

"Unfortunately, you're not privy to the bigger picture, or you'd realize that it's just *because* they've pulled out all the stops on this one that it's imperative they pay the price by *not* getting what they want so badly.

"Tell me about this bigger picture." Dane expected some standard need-to-know parry.

"How would you like to live in an energy-depleted world held hostage by an immoral international conglomerate that holds the reins of cheaper power but only doles it out to you—to me—or to anyone—on the basis of what *you* can do *for them* in return? Would prevention of that be worth the sacrifice of one woman?"

"No." Dane didn't have to think twice on that one—it was a no-brainer—and it had nothing to do with the woman being Helen.

"This is exactly why I'm here to make the critical decision for you." Gregory reached for the phone on the table that adjoined his chair. "Would you get me room two-one-three, please," he said to the operator. He waited to be connected, and then spoke to the other end: "I think we're ready for you to join us." That completed, he hung up.

"Look Gregory," Dane tried again, "Helen is just a tourist who's in this mess through no fault of her own."

"You may be happy to know that we've made it a point to confirm she is, indeed, just that. There was momentary speculation, among certain parties, that she might be more: for instance, a plant sent by The Mentlic Group to lead you down the proverbial garden path, ring through your nose."

"Helen? The enemy?"

"It does suggest a certain naiveté on your part that the idea never seems to have crossed your mind." Gregory gave an accompanying: *"Tsk-tsk!"*

There was a knock at the door, and they were joined by two men.

"Gentlemen," Gregory greeted, "may I introduce Dane who has, thus far, performed admirably in our employ; it very important we help him, now, maintain his impeccable service record. Dane, this is Tyler and Sampson."

The latter was well-suited to his moniker. Not only was his curly, sand-colored hair long enough to overlap his ears and his coat collar, but his body was obviously well-knit beneath double-knit. Tyler's nondescript medium height, thinning brown hair, and pale blue eyes, would have him easily lost in any crowd of more than five people.

Gregory focused again on Dane. "I suppose you wouldn't like to make it easier for us and just tell us where the stones are hidden?"

"You think my telling will make it easier for Helen?"

"You really must learn to widen your perspective, Dane." Gregory nodded to Tyler and Sampson in a go-ahead to begin their methodic search of the premises.

"I really would like to get dressed." Dane got sick to his stomach as the search moved closer to the prize.

"Yes, I imagine you would." This wasn't Gregory's permission for Dane to don anything.

Dane had only held the slightest hope that the mass of soaked and crumpled washrag at the bottom of the recently used shower would be distasteful enough to escape attention. He knew he'd hoped in vain when he heard the telltale clatter of released stones on the hard surface of the tiled shower floor.

"Ah, yes!" Gregory, too, heard, and it was music to his ears.

"It doesn't faze you that you've just signed Helen's death warrant?" Dane attempted to shame his boss.

"Of course it bothers me," Gregory surprised. "I wish there was someone to remove all this awesome responsibility from my shoulders, like Tyler, Sampson, and I, are here to do that very same favor for you. Because you, Dane, will look back on this and know that you did everything humanly possible, kept from buying Helen's life because of three men, one of whom held you at gunpoint to keep you from it. How much easier for you to get on with your life, knowing that—after this unfortunate interlude is over and done—you survive with a clear conscience."

"These what we want?" Sampson asked; the stones looked very small within the cupping of his massive hand.

Dane's confirmation was his rash leap to reclaim them. His towel came loose in the ensuing struggle, but he didn't care. If Gregory had gone to so much effort to explain how Dane could, after all of this, come to rationalize himself free of any blame, Dane had to be certain, even if it meant his life, that he'd exhausted every alternative.

His last-ditch effort of playing hero to Helen's heroine only got the life slowly being squeezed out of him by Sampson. Tyler was momentarily out of the action: a writhing heap left by Dane against one wall.

Gregory, in the end, decided when Dane's final indignation had played out far enough and ended it with the pistol barrel hard against the back of Dane's neck.

"Disappointing finale for you, Dane, to your otherwise job so well done!"

Dane was too deeply gone into complete unconsciousness to put any meaning to Gregory's parting comment.

CHAPTER FIVE

HIS HEAD FELT AS IF it was in a blender switched to *puree*. The intermittent ringing in his ears added to a pain that centered at the base of his skull and fanned out from there.

"Ohhhhh!" he indulged and was reassured that a dead man couldn't make such pitiful sounds.

He opened his eyes and, then, closed them when the resulting light was too much a stimulus to handle.

He lay there. Where? The surface beneath him was too hard for a bed. The floor was more likely. So, what was he doing on the floor?

The ringing stopped and began again. Signifying what? A concussion?

He opened his eyes, again, this time managing to keep them open in a painful squint. What he saw was a ceiling, the plaster cracked in a web-like design centered by a light fixture.

The ringing finally registered as most likely coming from a telephone somewhere above him.

He tried for a sitting position and succeeded. The blanket that Gregory had had the decency to rip from the bed, in parting, and throw over Dane's naked body, slid from Dane's neck to his lap. He took a fistful of the wayward material and modestly lifted it back. He made a concentrated effort to get to his feet.

He got as far as his knees before nausea swept through him. Only determination not to make a mess kept the surging bile locked in his throat.

The telephone stopped; the resulting silence was a welcome relief.

He made it from his knees to the bed. Face in hands, he survived another wave of sickening dizziness. He even managed to answer the phone on its next bout of ringing, but not out of any conscious effort to speak to whomever was on the other end. It was a defensive move to shut the damned thing up. He buried it in the blanket in his lap, and the resulting voice that came to him was very distant and tinny, a miracle of acoustics.

"Helen?" he asked the air, but this wasn't a conference-call phone that picked up conversation from a distance.

"Dane? Dane?" She repeated it several more times before he managed the connection of mouthpiece and receiver to his lips and ear.

"Helen?" he tried again.

"It *is* you!" she insisted. "I was sure they'd played some monstrous joke."

"You mean Red?" he attempted to put a name to at least one of the mysterious *they*.

"Red?"

Dane sifted his jumbled thoughts. "Red hair, khaki shirt and shorts. From the train."

"Oh, *not* him! I haven't seen him since I shot at him on the mountain."

"Darold Wesley, then?" That *drug-their-stew, fake-U.C.L.A.-student,* who had masqueraded as an *I'm-an-amateur-archaeologist-backpacker*, had better stay out of Dane's way. If Dane had doubts as to whether he was presently able to take on Red or Gregory, he was confident he could still cream Darold Wesley, and Dane would surrender his presently considerable bank account for the chance to do so.

"Yes. Darold gave me your phone number and put me in a car. Two men drove me, here, to the airport."

"You're actually at the airport?"

"I wanted to thank-you."

"Thank *me*?" Had she suffered a blow to her head, like he had? Someone who had screwed up her chances for living by losing the stones to Gregory was the last person she should thank.

"I imagine Dayklan really got on your case when they found out," she elucidated.

"Found out?" He sounded like Little Sir Echo and wished he could get his act together.

"That you ransomed me with the stones."

Was the lady crazy? Gregory and Dayklan, Tyler and Sampson, had the stones. None of whom had likely instigated any exchange; Dane had a nasty bump on his head to prove it.

"Dane, are you there?"

"I'm here."

"Something's wrong, though?" She didn't have to be a psychic to know their conversation was out of kilter.

"Who exactly told you that I gave The Mentlic Group the stones?"

"Darold, when he unlocked the door to this room where they'd kept me. Told me I was lucky that I'd gotten you to care so much for me in the few hours I'd known you. Walked me to the car. Drove me, here, to the airport. Handed me your hotel phone number and exchange. Said you'd be glad to hear from me before I flew away. Are you?"

She had every reason to be confused; *he* was confused.

"Is Darold there with you, now?"

"He didn't come in. Nor did his two associates."

"You're at the airport, now, alone? Is that what you're saying?"

"Alone if you don't count a few hundred people waiting for connections or baggage. Dane…?"

He didn't have time to guess at any explanation. He definitely needed time.

"Stay put, Helen, and I'll come to you. Where in the airport are you, exactly?"

"Almost directly across from the Faucett ticket counter."

"You say the area is crowded?"

"Pretty much so, yes."

"Good. Make sure there are always plenty of witnesses in case anyone decides to grab you."

"Why would they want me back?"

A better question: *Why had they let her go in the first place?*

"I'll be there as soon as I can."

He hung up and got dressed, pleased he could perform those basic tasks, even if his mind was less coordinated at the moment.

Gregory had left Dane's gun behind, Gregory not having been there with any real purpose of stockpiling munitions. A quick once-over of the weapon assured Dane it was still loaded and functional. He pocketed it and spent time at the elevator wondering if he'd be struck by another debilitating wave of dizziness.

He caught a cab out front. *"Aeropuerto."*

If they had set some kind of trap, they'd be hard-pressed to pull it off in a location that had upgraded security as a result of a recent terrorist attack that had killed twelve British tourists at a boarding gate.

On the spur of the moment, though, he had the cab driver pull up to a tobacco shop. He went inside to make a call, because it struck him as possible, now that he had a bit more of his wits about him, that someone merely jerked his chain; Helen wasn't at the airport at all.

"Would you, please, page outgoing Faucett passenger, Helen Mallory?" he requested of the airline agent who answered.

He waited and didn't expect success. Helen turned loose just wasn't a feasible format for an enemy who killed at the drop of a hat.

Muffled sounds told him the phone was about to be put back into use. So did the familiar, *"Hello,"* from the other end.

"Helen?" He genuinely couldn't believe it.

"Dane, is there something wrong?"

"I just wanted to confirm you'd called from the airport."

"You figure they're somehow setting me up as bait? Why, when they already have what they want?"

But they didn't have it, did they?

"Just don't leave the airport, Helen."

He went back to the waiting cab.

"You in some kind of trouble, buddy?" the cabbie asked in heavily accented English.

"Me? No. Why?" He wasn't convincing.

"There's a car back there that stopped when we did. I think it followed us from your hotel."

Leave it to a cab driver to do the job Dane should have done. On the other hand, why should Dane expect someone to follow him now that he no longer possessed the stones? Or, didn't The Mentlic Group know that? Even if they didn't, why sucker him to the airport when it was one of the safest places around?

"Maybe I *am* in trouble," Dane admitted to himself as well as to the curious driver. "You have any ideas about how we can lose that tail?"

"Hey, man, I'm not into cops and robbers, right? Maybe you should just get out and walk?"

"Take me to the cathedral," Dane instructed, sat back and settled in. He'd get out and walk all right, but not until it was more to his advantage.

Just before he got to his destination, he fished out a wad of bills, leaned over the front seat, tore the money in half with a flourish, and put one half of it onto the seat beside the driver. "You want the matching half of that, you drop me at the cathedral and beeline from there to the Church of San Blas. Wait for me there."

"Maybe." The driver seemed dubious.

"You're not being paid for *maybe*s."

"How long am I supposed to wait for you?"

"As long as it takes for me to cover the distance to you on foot, plus the bit more time it'll take for me to lose our friend."

"Okay."

Dane got out and headed up the steps to attach himself to a group of American tourists. Simultaneously, he spotted and identified his tail.

Can't be! he judged. *Why would Gregory send Tyler to keep tabs when Gregory already had all Dane had to offer?*

If Dane couldn't figure it out, he was in no mood to oblige either Gregory or Tyler with any upcoming minute-by-minute accounting of his whereabouts.

"Built on the site of Virachcha's Palace," the Americans' tour guide expounded, "this cathedral is considered by many to be *the* epitome of combined Spanish Renaissance style and Indian stonemasonry in the Western Hemisphere. The building took almost one-hundred years to build and incorporates many stones quarried from the immense Inca fortress at Sasahuaman."

Dane took his sweet time until the part about *the famous Maria Angola bell, cast in 1659 from a mixture of gold, silver, and bronze, weighing a ton, and the largest bell in South America.* By the time of *its deep and melodic tone can be heard up to twenty-five miles away,* Dane was off and running.

Dane's advantages were in Tyler not having known he'd been spotted and in Tyler's conceit in believing that he *never would be* spotted. Dane's sudden bolt caught the man completely by surprise, and it was only pure luck that had him spot Dane's hurried exit through a side door invisible to Tyler's backup in the parked car out front.

Dane took a roundabout route to the Palace of the Admiral. All uphill, he paused to look back for Tyler. Satisfied he'd lost him, it was only a short distance farther to rendezvous with the cabbie. Now if only Dane's bribe had been sufficient to keep the driver's interest.

He was relieved to find the cab and driver waiting where they were supposed to be.

"*Aeropuerto?*" the driver asked when Dane climbed in.

"*Sí,*" Dane agreed and, without being asked, put the complementary pile of ripped bank notes on the seat by the driver.

Earning his keep, the driver maneuvered a maze of narrow streets before coming out on the road to the airport.

By the time Dane sighted the terminal, he was convinced Tyler was no longer an immediate irritant.

He produced more money and repeated the tearing that had worked before. This time, he needed a safety depository for his gun which he'd hidden under the seat. There was no way he'd get the weapon through the airport's security system.

As he left the gun and the taxi, he worried that this was the way someone had cleverly planned to separate Dane from his weapon. Then again, the effort seemed something better accomplished without, as a result, positioning Helen and Dane safely behind a security cordon designed to prevent terrorism.

He was relieved when he joined Helen within the protection of the complex. Although she had said she'd wait for him, he was frankly surprised to see her.

Oblivious to the glances that accompanied their reunion in the middle of the floor, they basked in the sheer joy of again holding to each other.

Her lips were delicious when she lifted them in invitation for the kiss he had no qualms about giving her.

"Is it over, then, Dane? Is it finally done?"

Didn't he wish he had a *yes* for that? Unfortunately, something told him it wasn't over, by a long shot, although he didn't have a clue where it went from there.

He decided that if *he* couldn't make the pieces fit, two minds were better than one. Helen was as sharp as a tack, and he hoped she was better at the existing jigsaw than he was. He pulled her off to one side and told her just how things were. If he hated to admit that he wasn't the rescuing white knight in shining armor she may have imagined, this wasn't any time for the ego trip required to spare his feelings. He wanted this mystery over; if fessing up to his inability to keep Gregory from the rocks meant that Helen might gain better insight into their situation, it was worth it. Lack of communication wasn't something he planned to let screw up their chances.

He mistook the confusion on her face for criticism of his inability to save her. As if hit by a bolt of lightning, he was struck dumb by how much he didn't want to lose this woman now that he'd found her again. If coming clean as to his inadequacies endangered their relationship, he had second thoughts about having been so damned candid.

Helen's reaction, though, proved merely deep thought and not condemnation. Apparently, she understood that perfection in people and places only existed in fairy tales. "I just don't see it," she said and waved away one of the young boys with cameras, found all over Peru, who snapped photographs of tourists and appeared later to sell the resulting images.

"Here, kid, scram!" Dane pulled out a low-denomination bill and handed it over. He took Helen's arm and guided her to a more secluded spot.

"It makes The Mentlic Group less *villain-in-black-hat,* doesn't it?" she decided. "Somewhat sullies Dyklan's assumed *white Stetson* persona in the bargain."

"You're sure Darold said *I*'d turned over the stones?"

She might have asked him how many times he needed to hear it, but she didn't. "That's what he said. Plus, he had your phone and room numbers to give me."

"How about I put you on the very next plane headed for anywhere in the States?"

"Sounds fine to me as long as you're in the seat next to me." It seemed obvious that she thought he intended *anything but.*

"I'd feel better with you safe and out of this," he confirmed for her benefit.

"You think *your* feelings are more important than *mine* in this? Just how do you think I'd feel, safe and sound, you here to face *neither-of-us-can-*

even-guess-just-what? I'd feel like a rat deserting a sinking ship."

"I need time to check with Gregory and see what he comes up with—if anything."

"Then, we'll *both* check with this Gregory. After you treat me to a decent meal. The only thing good I've had to eat in days has been that *delicious-but-debilitating* stew of Darold's; the less said about that drug-based recipe, the better."

He wasn't convinced that Helen shouldn't take that next plane. Maybe *he* would be smarter to get on the aircraft *with her*. Except, he never could abide loose ends, and there were plenty of those presently left hanging.

"No matter what we find, it's bound to be between Dayklan and The Mentlic Group, now, isn't it?" Helen assured. "We're obviously out of the loop. How could we get dragged back in when Dayklan isn't likely to be impressed if The Mentlic Group offers one, or both, of us, at this point, in exchange for the stones? If The Mentlic Group wants to play nasty, there's an easier way than turn me loose and reel me in again."

"There's a game called cat and mouse, ever hear of it?"

"For us still to be mice in this game, here and now, doesn't *really* seem all that likely, does it?"

"People can be petty and vindictive. The Mentlic Group is made up of people who don't like the short end of any stick, especially when they're convinced this whole stick is rightly theirs."

"But how can they blame us when you were prepared to deal? Was it your fault Gregory barged in?"

Dane was ill at ease when they exited the terminal. His weapon in the cab, he waved both forward into the loading/unloading area. There was no need for him to ask after Helen's pistol; he'd left it empty on the mountain after fishing Darold's message from its barrel.

No doubt about it, Dane expected some move made against them before they entered the taxi. His relief in being wrong was a tangible thing that joined them. However, it wasn't a real relief he felt until he retrieved his gun from beneath the seat and verified it was loaded and viable as a defensive weapon.

"It looks as if the impossible has happened." His comment was spontaneous. He turned to Helen in the shadows beside him. "I just wish I were in some way confident of the *why*."

"Maybe beggars shouldn't be choosers?" She leaned forward in the seat and gave the driver the name of a restaurant. She settled back, pushed an arm between Dane and the seat and leaned her head against his shoulder.

"You were serious about being hungry."

"Wasn't I, though?" she admitted. "Actually, the word *famished* comes to mind. So, let's enjoy, shall we, and pretend for the next hour or so that we're just ordinary tourists?"

"I can live with that." He returned her hug and buried his face in her hair.

Despite his agreement to play at normality, his tainted perspective was revealed when he insisted the taxi wait while they ate; he just felt safer with reliable transportation on the ready, even if it was unlikely Helen and he would ever reach it if the enemy really had mind-set against it. To keep the driver happy, he provided the missing halves to the bills last ripped and provided some new halves. Helen's comment on the precaution was her supportive hug as they opened the door of the restaurant and entered the friendly warmth inside.

It was a small and definitely neighborhood eatery. It had rickety furniture, white paper table coverings, and paintings on the walls that never had been, and never would be, good enough to peddle even to gullible tourists on some street corner. The floor was hard-packed dirt. The three customers in residence were locals by the looks and by snatches of their conversation. The proprietor appeared through the bead curtain that separated the sparse eating area from the cluttered kitchen. He spoke English: a surprise to Dane. He knew Helen: another surprise to Dane.

"Ah, *Señorita* Mallory, welcome back!"

"Carlos, I'd like you to meet a dear friend of mine: Mr. Wilcox."

"*Señor* Wilcox, *Señorita* Mallory, this way, please, to my very best table."

"This place highly recommended by a gourmand acquaintance of mine in San Francisco who usually keeps such gastronomical discoveries a secret," Helen told Dane.

Carlos seated them and produced one menu which Dane assumed they were expected to share; he was wrong.

"The *señorita* will, of course, have the *cebiche de corvina, sí*?"

"*Sí.*"

"Trout a specialty of the house?" Dane questioned her selection.

Helen laughed. "I'm embarrassed to admit that I've eaten trout all through Peru. You remember that novel, revolving around Machu Picchu, which I told you brought me to Peru in the first place? Trout was what the romantic hero, Dane Green, was eating when he first met up with mysteriously dark and handsome, Sloane Hendriks; the latter definitely not in Peru as a tourist."

"She proceeded to blush an attractive pink that revealed itself only inadvertently by making her tan darker.

"Ah!" Dane returned her smile. "And did Sloane opt for the trout, too?"

"Actually, he ordered *conchitas* of tiny scallops, and *anticuchos* of chicken livers, shish-kebab."

"Sounds good by me. Are those available?"

"*Sí.*" Carlos confirmed.

"So be it, then!" Dane proclaimed.

Carlos retreated into the hidden recess of the kitchen and left Helen in a state of giggles from which it took her several seconds to recover. "As I remember, Sloane never finished his meal and left early, stiffing Dane with the bill."

"Well, if you insist...."

"Don't you dare!" she protested.

He had no intentions of going anywhere. The more he saw of Helen, the more he wanted never to leave her.

They spent an enjoyable couple of hours indulging in small talk that concentrated on the food (delicious!), the drinks (bottled water), and the reason for Dane Green and Sloane Hendrix having been in

Peru (the former to photograph Machu Picchu for a newspaper; the latter on a clandestine mission to recover a fortune in lost emeralds).

The magic was only partly diminished when it was time for the reality of the awaiting taxi in the outside evening darkness, and the pistol going more and more uncomfortable between Dane's Levi waistband and his meal-expanded stomach.

"Think your hotel has a spare room?" Helen made herself comfortable against Dane in the backseat of the cab. "I'm without suitable accommodations at the moment."

"I think something can be arranged." He tightly arm-wrapped her and pulled her close.

Their contentment remained until his hotel was only a couple of blocks away. Even then, it wasn't any sense of direct threat that had him glance at the three cars, in obvious caravan, that swiftly passed them. It was a freak of the nighttime lighting, of which Cuzco had really very little, that made Gregory temporarily visible within the backseat of the third vehicle.

Automatically, Dane slouched deeper and drew Helen down along with him.

Immediately, he'd metamorphosed from suitor to protector.

"Dane?"

Up the street, Gregory's car and the two others beat Dane and Helen's taxi to the Hotel Savoy."

Dane told his cabdriver to pull immediately to the curb.

The driver obeyed.

"What is it?" Helen whispered her concern.

"Those three cars, emptying their scurrying occupants, up there, in front of my hotel," Dane told her. "Gregory still sits in one of them."

It didn't take a script to follow what happened next. A couple of the men positioned themselves to each side of the hotel entrance. A couple more men disappeared around back. Two other men, one of whom Dane recognized as Sampson, disappeared inside.

Alone, Dane might have attempted to move in for a closer look. As it was, Helen made herself known to him by an increased rate of breathing that kept Dane right where he was.

Sampson reappeared shortly in a beeline for the car where Gregory waited. A minute later, he moved into concealment among the shadows in front of the hotel, and Gregory's car, Gregory inside, drove away.

"Follow that car!" Dane didn't care if he sounded like some character in a B-movie. His request was suitably succinct and fit the bill.

Helen didn't have to be told that their drive by the hotel required her to slide even deeper into her seat. She stayed low-profile, Dane equally as scrunched beside her, until it was safe for them to resume more upright positions.

They followed Gregory to a hacienda on the outskirts of Cuzco.

"I want you and the driver to wait for me here," Dane instructed when the taxi stopped.

"While you do what?" Helen wanted her suspicions spelled out.

"While I try and discover why I find Gregory's reappearance so disconcerting."

He expected her to protest and felt silly when she didn't; he kept forgetting this extraordinary young woman was his match in analyzing any situation.

She unscrewed the inside light that would have gone on when the taxi door opened. "Do be careful."

Dane headed for a lilac bush that latticed part of the wall that surrounded the hacienda grounds. He used its branches to make the top of the wall. Glass shards had once projected upward from the ledge of reached masonry, but they'd since broken off to leave only a few effective cutting edges.

Dane heard no dogs or guards, but that didn't mean they weren't there.

Completely dark when Gregory arrived, the house now had one light on downstairs. If Gregory had company, in any but that one lit room, they were hopefully asleep elsewhere.

A car went by a few streets away, its headlights fractured on the buildings and shrubbery in between.

The front door suddenly opened; Dane reflexively merged with the landscape.

He wasn't pleased that Gregory might leave so soon. He'd assumed this was home base and that the man would settle in for the night.

It wasn't Gregory who came out, though. Dane didn't have a clue who the guy was who got into the parked and drove it away.

Dane kept low in shrubbery that had been better manicured in former days.

He wasn't impressed by security. Still no sight of four- or two-legged guards. No sign of electronic

surveillance. Infrared triggering mechanisms? Maybe. More likely, though, there were so few trip
mechanisms because the stones were already en
route to wherever it was they were headed after having, just maybe, stopped off here.

Gregory was in the living room, spotted through
bars, dirty glass, and a large hole in parenthesizing
drapes. Dane couldn't see the whole room, but
Gregory *seemed* alone, bubble-glass of brandy in
hand, seated in a large winged-back chair.

The upstairs widows weren't barred. Dane used
a drain pipe as an elevator, and ended up accessing
the house via second-floor balcony French doors
with a broken lock. The bedroom he entered was
empty. The hallway beyond was empty, too.

It was dark, but Dane made out furniture that,
like the grounds outside, had seen better times.
Tufts of horse-hair stuffing blossomed from tattered
upholstery. The carpet was threadbare. The air
smelled musty. Nondescript pictures, of only
slightly better quality than those hung in the restaurant, tilted precariously on every wall. Curtains were
in shreds.

A phone rang downstairs.

Gregory's voice, faint but distinct: "No sign of
him yet?"

A receiver slammed on its hook.

Dane reached the stairs. Below, a swath of pale
light spilled from the living room onto the dusty
carpet of the hall.

A car pulled up outside, and Dane drew back
into deeper shadows. Gregory appeared and opened
the front door before any door bell rang or knocker
sounded.

Sampson entered.

"Something?" Gregory eagerly took the offered manila envelope and slid out its contents. He disappeared with the photographs into the living room that was obviously better lit to see them. Sampson followed.

Dane wanted to move closer, but he would become more vulnerable on the stairs.

"And our source for these?" Gregory asked. "The same anonymous *someone* who obliged us with the others?"

"So it seems," Sampson confirmed. "Notification and delivery procedures were the same."

"I'd be most interested to know their game. I remain suspicious of something for nothing."

"Maybe they're gloating," Sampson suggested.

Gregory continued: "Are we certain these are recent?"

"There's a newspaper in a couple of the shots. Read by that guy propped against the edge of the Faucett ticket counter."

Gregory's fist hit the top of a table with a bang. "I can't believe I let Dane pull a fast one."

"He certainly fooled me, too. How were we to know?"

"It's our job to know."

"What now?"

"Now, *you* go upstairs and get Tyler. If he'd kept track of Dane until we had the confirmation we needed, we'd not be scampering around now."

Dane executed a quick retreat; his noises were muffled by Sampson's as that man came barreling up the stairs two at a time. Dane couldn't reach a room in time, so he squatted behind one end of a moldy sofa scooted against a dark hallway wall.

Luckily, the room Sampson wanted was directly at the top of the stairs. He banged twice on its door, called Tyler twice, opened the door and went in. Only then did the room light come on, Sampson framed in the doorway.

"Up and at it, Tyler! We have an affirmative that Dane definitely pulled a switch-a-roo. Gregory wants us downstairs."

"I need a minute to piss," Tyler pleaded.

"Make it a quick one," Sampson warned. "You know how big this is to have gone down the toilet."

Sampson headed back downstairs. Dane waited a few seconds before he walked silently to the door that Sampson had left ajar. A second later, he walked on through it.

Tinkling sounds from the toilet said Tyler wasn't yet finished doing what he was doing in the bathroom. All Dane had to do was wait and, then, step to one side with an accompanying whack of gun butt to the back of Tyler's head when the man returned to the bedroom. This was exactly what Dane did. After which, he quickly intercepted the falling body at its armpits and eased its collapsing mass to the floor: a superfluous precaution in a building's whose primitive plumbing supplied sounds that would have masked any resulting thud of unconscious man to whatever the accepting surface.

Tying Tyler, in case of the man's untimely recovery, proved more of an inconvenience. The man wore loafers, affording no shoestrings. Nor did he wear a tie. Dane's next choice, a curtain sash, was rotten and disintegrated on touch. It was Tyler and Dane's belts that finally got the chore done.

"Tyler, get a move on!" Sampson demanded impatiently from downstairs.

This made stealth unnecessary when Dane finally headed down.

If he could have recorded Gregory and Sampson's expressions, upon seeing his arrival, his gun drawn, he would have jumped at the chance.

"You? How? Are you crazy?" Sampson sputtered.

Gregory was more articulate, but his sentiments were the same. "Whatever possesses you to come here? I credited you with enough sense to have you and your girl friend somewhere far safer by now."

"You expected me to leave the mystery, then?"

"Mystery?" Gregory didn't seem to think there was one.

"The one that brings you and your men to my hotel when you already have what you want. The one made deeper by certain snatches of conversation I've overhead here this evening. The mystery upon which, I hope, to shed some light by a look at those photographs from the manila envelope Sampson turned over to you earlier."

"You'll not extract yourself from this by merely feigning ignorance," Gregory warned. "That you figure us so dumb that you even make the effort is insulting and won't make you any friends."

Without invitation, Dane stepped to the desk to see the pictures Gregory had scattered there. "Helen and I at the airport?"

"That's what they look like to me, too," Gregory agreed.

From some of the angles, the pictures had likely been taken by the *kid-with-camera* Dane had hustled away with a bribe.

"You should have gotten a plane while you had the chance," Sampson defined it the way he saw it.

"So what that I met Helen at the airport? I was glad, through no help from you or me, that she ended up safe and sound, there."

"You got that only half right," Sampson amended.

"What's that supposed to mean?"

"Cut the charade, Dane!" Gregory commanded. "Whatever your game, we aren't playing it any longer. Even without those photographs to prove you gave The Mentlic Group the stones to ransom Helen, we had the resources available to identify, eventually, the decoys you cleverly hid in your shower."

"Decoys?"

"Worthless basalt!" Sampson filled in.

"You're lucky Dayklan isn't as vindictive as its competition," Gregory congratulated, "Or you'd end up dead for this betrayal. You can bet, though, your life will be made very difficult in the years you have remaining. Unless, of course, you're here to tell me you've pulled another fast one and ransomed Helen with more bogus stones."

"I don't know what you're trying to pull, Gregory, but what you got was what I went through a helluva lot of bother to get this far."

"Basalt doesn't register anywhere near blood-red resolution, Dane," Gregory reminded. "What's that tell you?"

"That Roger passed me the wrong stones at Machu Picchu?"

"That he ended up dead for his efforts indicates to me that you're wrong in that assumption."

"I don't care what it indicates *to you*." Not true! "Maybe Roger picked the wrong stones up on site?"

"He was a trained geologist, for Christ's sake!" Sampson obviously didn't for a moment believe Dane's fumbling grab for some kind of other explanation. "He had a portable spectrometer along with him to tell him *exactly* what he saw."

"He jettisoned the spectrometer," Dane remembered.

"Was that before or after he used it to make his selection?" Gregory smiled wryly.

"I tell you, the stones you got from me were the ones he handed over."

"Well, excuse me if I find that hard to believe until you come up with as much proof as we have proof of a double-cross to the contrary. While you're looking at pictures, why don't you open the top middle drawer of the desk and tell me what you think of the ones in there?"

Dane opened the drawer only after his fingers checked for any booby trap.

"You really are photogenic," Gregory accompanied Dane's final unveiling of the drawer contents. "No mistaking you as a passenger on that bus, is there? As for the gentleman seated next to you, he's been identified as Cleveland *Red* Clanburger, a trouble-shooter The Mentlic Group has used more than once in their nefarious dealings."

"I thought your man didn't spot me until the bus depot in Cuzco?" Dane remembered the overheard

comments made by Gregory about the suspicious-
ness of the anonymous donor. Gregory's failure to
make an immediate response told Dane to make the
most of it. "So, who snapped me on the bus with
Cleveland *Red* Clanburger? And why would you get
rushed copies unless in a setup to discredit me?"

"Discredit you to what purpose?" Gregory was
prepared to listen.

"Out of pure spite for The Mentlic Group having been bested."

"But if they didn't get the stones, and we didn't
get the stones, and you profess not to have the
stones, where do *you* propose they've gotten to?"

"Sprouted little legs and feet to walk off on, no
doubt," Sampson suggested with sarcasm.

Dane knew of one *until-now-unthought-of* alternative. There was the possibility Helen hadn't been
as far gone as he'd imagined when, on the Inca
Road, Darold having drugged them, Dane had fran-
tically hidden the specimens beneath that lean-to
masonry. Except, he refused to believe that! He
knew a helpless tourist, drawn unwittingly into the
game, as opposed to a seasoned player. Hell, even a
thorough investigation by Dayklan had, according to
Gregory, left Helen clean. If Darold had forced the
information out of her, or even used truth serum to
get at it, Helen would have surely remembered
enough to mention it after the fact.

"Where *are* the stones you swiped from my
bathroom?" Dane demanded of Gregory.

"If you're trying to insinuate that *I'm* out to pull
some kind of fast one…?" Gregory wasn't allowed
to finish.

"Where?" Dane insisted.

"In the basement, why?"

"I want to see them as soon as you tie up Sampson." Their shoes were more obliging with shoelaces that Tyler's loafers had been.

"You aren't going to prove anything by seeing those rocks again!" Sampson protested as Dane oversaw the securing of the man's wrists and ankles. "Why don't you cut the act, collect your mistress, and hightail it out of here while the going is even marginally good?"

Dane silenced him with a hard rap of gun butt to the back of the man's head.

"Sampson's advice was only for your own good," Gregory argued. "You ought to think seriously about following it."

"At the moment, I'm following you into the basement. Can you assure me that there aren't any booby traps or people lying in wait?"

"You seem to have Sampson and I momentarily under control."

"You wouldn't like to mention Tyler, would you?"

Gregory was a fast thinker. "I assumed you entered the house from a second-floor window and took out Tyler on the way down."

"Don't make any other assumptions."

"We're quite alone."

"I hope for your sake that's true. Now, if you'd show me the way to the basement."

"Do you really expect...?"

"What I expect is for you to show me to the basement," Dane interrupted.

The journey was out of the living room, down the hallway, through the kitchen to the basement door.

A light switch turned on the lone bulb that illuminated the stairway adequately for Dane to keep close tabs on Gregory all of the way down.

"Satisfied?" Gregory resumed conversation in a large room self-contained enough to hold no obvious surprises.

"So, where are they?"

"You will recognize them won't you, Dane? I mean, they look common enough to the uninitiated, but you've had a few days to get to know them. They're old friends, yes?"

"Where?"

"On the counter, over there." Gregory nodded in the desired direction. "Hardly valuable enough to keep under lock and key."

"You make one wrong move, and you're dead meat."

He went over and confronted, with simultaneous relief and anxiety, the proof-positive that Helen hadn't pulled any switch when she'd had the opportunity to do so; the stones he saw on the counter were definitely the ones he'd carried the distance. He knew the one's peculiarly beveled edge, the other's erratically granulated surface, the last's sharp facet. No way could Helen, or anyone, have easily duplicated them so exactly on such short notice.

"Shouldn't you now accuse Dayklan and me of duplicity in a plot to paint you the villain of the piece?" Gregory's voice oozed sarcasm.

"These *are* the specimens Roger gave me."

"They are, also, common basalt. They, also, are *not* blood-red resolution matrix."

"That your portable spectrometer?" Dane indicated the piece of nearby electronic equipment.

"You really needn't proceed with this charade of innocence for my benefit," Gregory said.

"Shut up and tell me where you keep the master graph for blood-red resolution matrix."

Gregory nodded to a file cabinet.

"Get it *and* the master graph for basalt."

"Why dig your hole any deeper, Dane? You've admitted the stones are the ones you let us find in your shower. Match a master graph for basalt with yet another spectrometer readout on the stones, and where does that put you? In a corner, yes? Or, will it be back to making Roger the scapegoat?"

"Just do it!"

Taking Gregory's word as to the duplication of results would have saved Dane a good deal of time and effort.

"See," Gregory insisted when the verdict was in. "The spectrometer never lies."

"Someone switched master graphs." Dane could think of no other explanation.

"A possibility, I suppose." Gregory didn't sound convinced.

"Turn around."

"Don't do anything to make Dayklan madder at you than it is already, Dane."

"Turn around!" He was suddenly worried about time. If Gregory had a fixed schedule, now violated, how long would it take for his people to investigate? How much longer would Helen be content to wait without coming to find out what had happened to Dane?

He used his gun to knock Gregory out. He was becoming quite the expert at beanings, lately. He hoped he had it down well enough so that he wasn't delivering concussions in the bargain. It wasn't as if he had any alternative. He didn't want these people making waves until he was safely away from them.

The basement proved a better source of bindings than upstairs. Dane used from a convenient cache of electrical wiring.

Then, he folded the master graphs for basalt and blood-red resolution matrix and stuffed them into his shirt. He fitted the portable spectrometer into its leather carrying case.

He climbed the basement steps and turned out the light behind him.

CHAPTER SIX

THE HIRAM BINGHAM ROAD meandered familiarly up the mountain. Its snaky curves spewed dust beneath the wheels of the vans that crazily moved the swarm of tourists to the gray ruins.

Dane and Helen didn't leave the train. They were going farther this time.

Neither was surprised by Gregory's arrival. They stayed seated, their packs and the portable spectrometer on the rack above them. Their guns were secured at the smalls of their backs, and they left them there.

"I'm expected, am I?" Gregory divined.

"Came by helicopter, did you?" Dane adjusted his position on a first-class seat that definitely needed more padding for any kind of real comfort.

Helen motioned Gregory to take the empty seat across from them.

"I wasn't up to the rigors of the train ride," he admitted. "I've this headache from something having recently hit my head."

"I presume you weren't tied and gagged for too long." Dane checked for Gregory's men and finally spotted Sampson and Tyler on the platform outside.

"Not long," Gregory admitted.

"As soon as I left, your rescuers came out of the woodwork, did they? From somewhere in the house?"

"Secret rooms," Gregory confirmed. "The hacienda is riddled with them."

"Since I last saw you, Helen and I had a chance to think things through. We decided your raid on my Savoy Hotel room was too obvious, and your true home base would have been better secured."

Helen nodded agreement.

"You make an excellent team, you two," Gregory complimented.

"You suckered me," Dane accused.

"Only for your own benefit, in that I wanted to be sure you were the man I'd always thought you were. As you know, I was suspicious from the get-go of those accusatory photos dropped on my doorstep, no one asking for anything in return. I wanted to hear what you had to say about them. I still haven't all the pieces, but you at the house, and you here, argue powerfully in your favor. You *are* off to get me real samples, right?"

Dane and Helen nodded in unison.

"That tells me, even if you did somehow screw up, you're making amends. This is how I'd expect a professional to act. Not to mention how it's the quickest way to extradite all of us from our present mess. We've been left with too much egg on our collective face. Selecting and bringing in someone other than you, let alone bring him up to speed, at this point, would only consume valuable time we possibly can't spare."

"You traveled all this way, then, to put our minds at ease and give us a pep talk?" Dane hoped for more.

"You'll have a hard enough time without thinking we're sneaking up on you from behind. I'm here to reassure you that won't be the case."

"And we hope that you're here, too, to deliver certain coordinates," Helen prodded. "There's a lot of jungle out there in which to pinpoint, even with a portable spectrometer, one small patch of ground."

Gregory pulled a folded paper from his pocket and handed it over.

The conductor announced the train was about to leave. Gregory didn't move.

"Coming along for the ride?" Dane asked. "The more the merrier."

"Only as far as Timilizic, I'm afraid. The chopper's waiting for me there. I can, by the way, Helen, arrange for you to be flown immediately to the safety of Cuzco."

"Not bloody likely," Helen declined.

Dane's look asked her to reconsider. Her look remained obstinate, and he didn't elaborate upon his continuing concern for her safety. Gregory's response was an accepting shrug.

"The train strained to start, its attempts ragged at best.

"I seriously thought of accompanying you all of the way in," Gregory confessed, "but my superiors said I was too old for that sort of thing."

"*I'm* too old for that sort of thing," Dane wasn't at all reluctant to admit.

"I'm here, then, to protect your rear," Gregory explained. "It's important, yes, that you have someone waiting who you can trust enough to turn over the new samples if—when—you get them?"

The last of the vans were up the mountain. Ant-like people swarmed the thatched rest station over-hanging the valley.

"It's only fair, too, that I tell you the latest rumor," Gregory resumed after a pause. "Every bit of input helps, yes?"

"Are we talking good news or bad?" Helen had a premonition it was the latter.

Gregory produced a photograph from his shirt pocket. "Care to check a picture that doesn't include either of you for a change?" He handed it to Dane who reached for it. "The man is Douglas Symphel, The Mentlic Group's man in Chile. The ship is Liberian registry. The port is Valparaiso. The canister is believed to contain plutonium that has since been successfully smuggled overland to where you're headed."

"The stuff used to make A-bombs?" Helen was aghast.

"Mmmmmm," Gregory hummed affirmation. "Weapons'-grade *is* the prevalent scuttlebutt."

"They're making a nuclear device?" Dane jumped to his own conclusion.

"Not exactly," Gregory qualified. "No need for such complicated busywork if they've a non-nuclear bomb available. Which we suspect they do."

"I don't understand," Dane and Helen chimed in harmonic duet.

"The plutonium needn't go critical to do its intended job. It only need be scattered physically to contaminate the area for the next 300 years or so. A large enough conventional bomb can do that trick if they should ever come to think the site again compromised. Unfortunately, your arrival on the scene just might be considered such a compromise."

"How would they explain such a catastrophe?" Helen wanted to know.

"Who says they'd have to explain it?" Gregory argued. "Who's to believe, except a knowledgeable few of us, that a legitimate company could be so covetous of some out-of-the-way stretch of Peruvian wilderness that they'd operate on an *if-I can't-have-it-no-one-can* mentality? More likely, blame will successfully be laid on some terrorist splinter group fiddling for nuclear capability. Do you know how much plutonium turns up missing from points of origin, during the course of any given year, terrorists held responsible?"

"If The Mentlic Group is so afraid we'll gain access, why not blow the area now?" Dane was prepared to milk his information source for all it was worth.

"Conjecture has it that they hold out hopes of getting as much of the deposit as possible mined and smuggled out of Peru to supplement their Guatemala find."

"Only two known deposits on the face of the Earth and The Mentlic Group are prepared to contaminate one of them?" For some reason, Helen found that more than a tad far-fetched.

"A deposit not in their control might as well not exist, according to their way of thinking. They're in a holding pattern, no hope for legal control of this site, because of their soiled past history in Peru. The Dayklan-Peruvian deal is foreordained, merely a question of finances, *after* we know definitely what we've got, whether we can exploit it to some advantage The Mentlic Group obviously thinks we can, and whatever our potential for profit has already apparently been computed by them."

"What hope do we have to get control of the bulk, even if we get you a preview?" Helen didn't want Dane or her lives risked for nothing.

"All the facts in, a concentrated effort can be launched. For the right price—presently still too exorbitant until we can be assured suitable returns—people can be hired, professionals prepared to take whatever the risks of getting anything from anybody."

"I still can't figure where Roger's sampling went wrong." Dane found no consolation in probably never knowing.

"Unfortunately, the only man who can clear that up to anyone's satisfaction is Roger." Gregory's comment was superfluous; Dane and Helen had seen Roger's body.

When the train pulled into Timilizic, Gregory made one last effort to entice Helen to fly to safety in Cuzco. His offer this time, like the last time, likely wasn't entirely humanitarian but based more upon background-investigation results which had revealed Helen with nothing in her previous life to prepare her for something like this. On the other hand, Dane had spent three years in the U.S. Army, assigned to Special Force's *Phi-Omni* which had seen covert action in the Colombian government's war against the Medellin drug cartel. If Dane's *Phi-Omni* stint had changed his mind about his suitability for lifer-status in the military, it *had* given him credentials enough to impress United Courier Ser-

vice into providing him to Dayklan for the rendezvous with Roger at Machu Picchu. His background
would, likewise, prove invaluable to him now.

"Last chance, Helen," Gregory reminded.

"I'm not going somewhere to sit on the side-
lines," Helen was adamant, "wondering what Dane
is up to. I've waited too long for this special man to
let him walk out for however long it's going to take
him to clear his good name with you people."

"Then, I'll wish you both good luck." There
were certain advantages, after all, in Dane having
Helen along. Her presence would make him consider his actions really carefully, lest he *and* she get
killed by his carelessness.

The train completed it last convulsive shudder to
a complete stop. Gregory disembarked.

Dane verged on encouraging Helen to pull out,
too, but she anticipated what he proposed and cut
him off at the pass. "I won't get in your way out
here, I promise. You tell me what to do in the field,
and I'll do it. Just don't tell me to get on any helicopter with Gregory, here and now."

Maybe Dane was selfish, but in counterpoint to
his desire to see Helen safely away, there was another part of him that wanted her along. Not because
he wanted the woman he now knew he loved to confront the dangers he knew were out there, but because he liked and enjoyed her company; he trusted
her judgment. Besides, if and when he ran across
members of the enemy who didn't have foreknowl-
edge of whom he was, he counted upon the presence
of Helen to be the convenient *brush* to paint him
and her more innocent than they actually were.

126

Half an hour later, the train made another stop. Its engine screeched into literal contact with the flank of one of three cows that had inadvertently wandered onto the tracks and refused to budge before the prolonged shrill screams of the train's whistle. Dane and Helen gathered their things to advantage the unexpectedly convenient moment for disembarkation from the train.

"If The Mentlic Group has watchers, they'll likely be posted at the scheduled stops positioned for best access to their claimed spot of jungle," Dane explained the obvious. "Who's to see us get off here?"

For two days, they heard or saw no one. Not all that unusual in that they were still pretty far from their destination to warrant retaliatory action by the enemy. That didn't mean they were slovenly in their security. Two people could alternate sleep-and-watch routines.

There were no indigenous locals, because a terrain that saw steep embankments rearing to the Inca Road, then immediately dropping off into deep gorges on the other side, wasn't well-suited for human habitation.

The sheer physical effort required of their own daily movements left them exhausted at the end of each day.

"I'm glad I had a modicum of acclimatization before I undertook this mission." Helen pushed her hair, dank and lank with dirt and perspiration, from her eyes and into better concealment beneath the brim of her safari hat. "Did I ever thank you for the trial run, the redheaded man in pursuit, along the Inca Road?"

Dane tossed her a bag of walnuts and raisins, high-energy food that didn't require stove or camp fire.

Helen particularly disliked the nights; Dane wasn't fond of them, either. There was something about daylight's reassurance that too quickly disappeared with nightfall. The darkness brought too many disconcerting sounds of animals, unseen, suddenly on the prowl.

"You know," Helen tried to put into words her emotions felt at the beginning of one watch, "it's no consolation whatsoever that our worst enemy, when and if he comes, won't likely make any noise at all."

Their next encounter with their *worst enemy* wasn't when or how they expected. As on the Inca Road, Darold, in *déjà-vu* materialization, merely appeared beyond one of the many turns of their trail.

Once again, he leaned on a rock for support. This time, he'd had better luck with his pipe which already spewed its pleasant cherry-wood tobacco smoke and aroma.

"Well, well, well!" He had no visible weapon, but it was unlikely he was where he was, when he was, without some means of offense and/or defense.

Automatically, Dane and Helen drew *their* guns.

"Not very neighborly," Darold viewed their mutual display of firepower.

Dane gave their immediate surroundings a quick once-over; Helen gave full attention to Darold.

"Oh, I'm quite alone at the moment," Darold assured. "When and if you meet me farther along, I'll undoubtedly have company and the benefit of booby traps. The latter really nasty things that can take out an eye, blow off a leg, make sure neither of you ever become loving parents."

"How did you find us?" Helen didn't need Darold's detailed dissertation to know what had to be avoided.

His laugh wasn't the kind that coaxed anyone to join in. "My dear Helen, we never lost you. Once you boarded the train in Cuzco, that is. And weren't we surprised to see you. Having been so generous in letting you go once, we thought you knew we weren't likely to be so considerate the next time. As it turns out, we *are,* though, prepared to be just as considerate; any third time, if you're foolish enough to test us, will definitely see you strike out. Take my word for it."

"You're here, then, to give friendly warning," Helen decided.

Darold apparently thought the answer too obvious to answer. He took another deep draw of his pipe, his jaw still bruised (and hurting?) from the blow it had received from Dane's pistol on the mountain, and proceeded to other things. "You know, I told them it might not be smart to go to all that childish bother to ruin Dane's reputation with Dayklan by making it appear he sold out to us by ransoming you, Helen. I said—and I quote myself verbatim: 'Dane isn't the sort who'll easily abide any slur to his honesty. This can cause all sorts of potential complications for us later.' My superiors, however, couldn't understand that by leaving Dane's reputation unsullied they might have prevented your present grandstand play. They only knew that Dayklan had the stones, when the whole purpose of the exercise was for Dayklan never to get close enough to know the stones were phony. Far more anxiety for Dayklan to believe they'd had the real things, only to lose them. Not that there wasn't plenty of anxiety to go around if and when your bosses learned they'd been duped from day one."

"How duped?" That's what Dane wanted to know.

"Listen carefully." Darold gave another puff of fragrant tobacco smoke. "This explanation should assure you that no one can fault you; you needn't proceed with this madness to prove anything to anybody."

"Get on with it!" Helen found his smug and patronizing attitude irritating beyond belief.

"Blame Roger Kimlery," Darold fixed the culprit. "Oh, he got the right stones originally. This, I might add, made more than a few people more than a little angry. But, I'm afraid that it was all downhill for him from then. We gave him a merry chase through the jungle, during which we captured his bodyguard."

"Jim Chimchuck," Dane identified.

"I do believe I did see a dossier with that name on it," Darold confirmed.

"Go on about Roger." Dane had seen the geologist alive before seeing him dead.

"Poor, deluded Roger actually thought he made it home free." Darold's smile was all amusement. "But the man was so mentally and physically drained by his flight through the jungle, accompanied by the constant sounds we supplied of Jim's ongoing torture, he was constantly experiencing spontaneous bits of sleep that lasted from one to several minutes. Medical science has a name for it."

His expression said he was trying to dredge up the terminology.

Dane didn't need explanations that specific. "You simply exchanged the stones while he slept?"

"For marvelous, undetected results, don't you agree?"

"So, why murder him at Machu Picchu?" Helen asked. "Why kill that harmless hiker at the hotel? Why shoot me in the arm? Why kill the courier on the train? Why wreck the train? Why kidnap me?"

"We needed time to solidify and fortify our position. We were still vulnerable when Roger stumbled on the scene; that no better illustrated than by how he obtained his samples before we detected or stopped him. We were moving toward a plan for impenetrable perimeters, but we needed time to put the plan into place. Roger not showing up at Machu Picchu would have told Dayklan the mission had failed, and Dayklan would have possibly launched another, immediate, attempt that we'd have had to devote time and energy to deflect or abort. Better for Dayklan to think Roger successful, the samples on the way, we out to stop delivery."

"You killed all of those people to buy time?" Helen was appalled.

"Every war has its collateral damage," Darold rationalized.

"War? War?" To Helen, his reasoning was incredulous. If it wouldn't have made her as bad as he was, she would have pulled the trigger and blown him away in disgust, right then and there. "You're talking people versus pieces of rock, here."

"What do you think wars are fought over, if not pieces of rock, Helen?" Obviously, Darold thought her naïveté feigned. "*Manifest Destiny* and *Westward Ho* caused wars with the American Indians. *Living Space* pushed Hitler into Europe and Russia."

"That's between nations." Not a suitable rebuttal and Helen knew it.

"You think Dayklan and The Mentlic Group aren't nations unto themselves? You should see their balance sheets, their holdings, their investment interests."

"What's so important to The Mentlic Group about this particular plot of dirt?" If Darold was talking, Dane figured to take every advantage.

"What's important about it is that it's ours. Our SIS pinpointed it. Our geologists dug it out. Our scientists discovered its potential. Dayklan is a *Johnny-come-lately*: the bully on the block out to steal the other kids' lunch money: the barnyard animal who didn't help the Little Red Hen plant the wheat, harvest the wheat, grind the wheat to flour, or mix the dough, but expects his share of the bread. Well, it's just not going to happen!"

"Nor would it even have a chance if your organization hadn't cheated Peru out of millions so Dayklan was handed friendly-partner status on a silver platter."

"What's in Peru belongs to Peru," Helen thought a far better perspective.

"Possession is ninety-nine percent of the law," Darold trumped. "And we've had the time, thanks to the past few days, to lock up full possession. If you don't believe me, proceed with your present course. When you fail, let Dayklan send in as many replacements as it pleases. No one is going to thank it; certainly not you or Peru."

Especially not if Dane, Helen, and a large chunk of the country ended up glowing radioactive, but neither Dane nor Helen said that. They didn't want to endanger the Dayklan information source. However, their discretion proved needless.

"We know Dayklan knows we brought in a canister of weapons-grade plutonium through Valparaiso," Darold said. He could tell his candidness took them back. "Surely, you didn't think we *wouldn't* know? Not when you've both experienced how we advantage certain photographs turned up on certain doorsteps. Had we meant the plutonium kept secret, rather than expected Dayklan to put two and two together, there would have been no camera within miles to record it."

Another possibility struck him.

"Or, maybe Dayklan conveniently forgot to mention to you that we'd smuggled in the plutonium as backup."

"We were told, all right," Helen nipped that conjecture in the bud.

"Oh?" He sounded disappointed. "Shall I tell you what that tells me about Dayklan and the two of you?"

"Do we have a choice?" Dane was facetious.

"It tells me the people at Dayklan aren't quite as unfeeling as I thought, although I suspect a softy like Gregory spilled the beans over the objections of his more cynical higher-ups. It tells me, no matter how feeling the people at Dayklan might be, they're not so much so—and this includes Gregory—that they did the sensible thing and kept you out of danger. Finally, it tells me you two have far less smarts than I've given you credit for, since you seem to have come this far knowing the potential cost to you and to Peru."

He shook his head: a disappointed father-figure.

"Don't think," he continued, "that you're marching in here at the forefront of a far better master than The Mentlic Group. You can quote me those millions out of which we bilked Peru, and I'll be hard-pressed to deny it. But do you know about the mismanagement of the Rilsen oil reserves by Dayklan? Do you know about the behind-the-scenes machinations that topped Soo Sook so Dayklan could access Asian nickel reserves?"

Once again, he shook his head.

"Go home, you two. Get married. Have babies. Live happily ever after. None of which will be possible if you continue this craziness that's motivated by your masters more interested in corporate greed than in you."

Finally finished, he nodded farewell and calmly walked off into the surrounding terrain like someone out for a Sunday stroll.

"Well!" That and her accompanying sigh was how Helen viewed Darold's visitation. Had he really just been there, plain as day?

Dane holstered his gun. "First off, I know for a fact that the mismanagement of the Rilsen oil reserves was the fault of a greedy local politician in cahoots with OPEC. Secondly, Soo Sook was toppled by a greedy nephew who had already made arrangements to give the nickel concession to The Mentlic Group before a counterrevolution put a stop to that bit of chicanery."

"You don't believe Darold, either, about the substitution of the fakes for the real stones while Roger slept?"

"It's certainly the best explanation to date. Will Dayklan believe it, though, enough to let me off the hook? What do we really have to prove any such substitution but Darold's say-so?"

"You want to go back, I'll go back with you. You want to go forward, I'll go forward with you. You want to propose marriage, I'll accept."

He wrapped her slim waist and pulled her close for a hug and a kiss. "Don't think I won't hold you to that once we're out of here and I'm clear to lead my life without Dayklan interference."

"It's onward, then?"

"What I'd like is a closer look to assure me that The Mentlic Group has the site as firmly sewed up as Darold says. I see *his* advantage in meeting us here to warn us and turn us away. It could keep any nastiness isolated from the site itself; it could keep him and his from the necessity of destroying the source if they don't have to. But it makes me suspicious that they want us returned to Dayklan with the story of a nut too hard to crack, when we haven't gotten close enough to see if the shell even has a weak spot."

"If Darold lied about the Rilsen oil reserves and the fall of Soo Sook, he could lie about this on-site security. Maybe the time they've already bought hasn't been enough to get the plutonium from Chile and into place, here, in Peru."

"Maybe."

"What can a few more hours on the trail hurt us, right?"

Trouble was, it could hurt them plenty.

It certainly had hurt Cam Reginal who entered their lives two hours and eleven minutes later with his grunt and groan that froze them on the spot and made them draw their pistols. His sounds were more animal than human, and Dane actually expected a jaguar lurked somewhere near. Cam's *in-a-heap* crumple in a medium growth of ferns wasn't the best indication of what or whom they'd found.

They approached with caution. Helen's, "It's a man!" finally put definition to the reality.

"Let's play this slow and easy." If it looked as if Cam were no immediate threat, Dane knew that looks could deceive. Dane used the toe of one boot to turn the man over.

Helen's gasp indicated the battered appearance of Cam's face which improved only slightly beneath Helen's follow-up ministrations with handkerchief and canteen water.

Cam attempted introductions several times during the course of Helen's first aid; it took him more than a few tries to wrap his split lips around any kind of decipherable discourse.

"You must be Helen and Dane," he managed finally.

"Do *we* know you?" Dane sure as hell didn't know him.

"Name's Cam Reginal. An acquaintance of yours said I should expect to run into you on my way out." He grimaced as a tic convulsed the left side of his face and painfully contracted a network of bruises and scratches. He said this—" He supported his chin with his fingertips to tilt his face in their direction. "—is the least of what you can expect for *your* ongoing efforts."

"*Darold* did this!" Helen didn't need a second guess.

Dane imagined the results of a similar brutal assault on Helen's attractive features. The way Cam's nose was adrift on his face, Dane suspected it was broken.

"Actually, the little dweeb sicced a bigger guy on me. Guy name of Red. Red is not anyone you'd care to meet in a dark alley."

"Apparently, Darold had this done to you as some kind of example to us." Dane had to admit, it was a show-and-tell visual aid that made the point.

"Not entirely." Cam managed a sitting position for the first time. He accepted Helen's handkerchief to staunch a renewed flow of blood from his nose. "Seems he had me figured for a claim jumper and decided I needed some discouragement of my very own."

"*Are* you a claim jumper?" It was Helen's way of finding out who he was and what he was doing where he was. She could tell, just by looking, that Dane remained suspicious, and he had every right to be. Darold wasn't beyond having one of his own men beaten up just to insert him into the enemy camp.

"Prospector," Cam identified. "I was up north, having had no luck whatsoever, and the jungle telegraph said someone had struck it really big down this way. I merely decided to head on down to take a look. It wasn't so much a case of planning to jump anyone's claim as it was a desire to latch, maybe, onto *some* piece of the action."

"Jungle telegraph?" Helen's mind flashed Tarzan movies with beating drums before she realized *those* were an ocean and continent away.

"Tim Simle first told me. He and I go back to when I first got to South America six years ago, and he was panning the headwaters of the Ipixuna. That's in Brazil." He managed to look nostalgic even through the distorted features of his beating. "I should have stayed in Brazil. So far, all I've gotten out of Peru is bad news."

"You were saying that this Tim recently told you someone around here made a big strike," Dane encouraged.

"Tim had a run-in with Darold, too?" Helen figured that wasn't any giant leap of logic.

"Not firsthand. Tim stuck around only long enough to tell from a distance that the guy had moved in enough firepower to keep what he'd found. Tim had sense enough to know trouble when he spotted it and headed for the Piedras. This is where I saw him. He advised me to keep my distance, but I've had nothing but lean pickings for so long, I figured it might be worth a little danger for the chance to pick up some of this guy's leavings. Not even Paul's infected hand warned me away."

"*Paul*'s infected hand?" Helen had followed the veer in conversation but wasn't sure how it connected.

"Paul Naxwen. He was only a few miles up the Apurimac when *he* got the word and decided to come in for a look-see of his own. Some kind of wooden spike came popping up on a spring mechanism and stabbed him clear through his hand. Nasty looking wound. Not something I'd want to try and

138

treat myself. Not something that'll likely heal easily in the deeper jungle where Paul's headed." Cam's fingertips once again tentatively explored the damage to his face.

"Darold has booby-trapped the area." Dane shouldn't have been surprised; Darold had said that was the case. Then again, Dane hadn't seen Paul's palm puncture, had he? How reliable a witness was Cam whose battered face looked really bad but, upon closer examination, consisted primarily of superficial wounds?

"Darold told me I was lucky he found me before *I* found any of his booby traps," Cam remembered. "'Count your blessings!' Was how he put it. 'Red will at least leave you able to walk away and carry on a conversation with Helen and Dane when you run across them.' We *did* decide that you *are* Helen and Dane?"

"In the flesh," Dane confirmed.

"You *did* successfully jump his claim on the Napo?"

"We did what?" Helen wasn't sure she'd understood; Cam still had problems with enunciation.

"Said he'd hit it big in Ecuador. A year of heat, bugs, and jungle rot, and he'd found gold in a stretch of the Napo. You two moved in and sent him packing. He won't be burned a second time, not by the same two people, to hear him tell it."

"Why that...." Helen didn't finish. There was a certain advantage to the cover story Darold had provided. If Cam was who he said he was, he was better off without the truth of the matter.

"Let me tell you from personal experience, you guys: Your friend is more than prepared for you this time."

Helen couldn't believe that she passed muster as someone who made her living traipsing the wilderness and snatching hard-won earnings from men who didn't surrender their pokes all that easily. Then again, she hadn't checked a mirror lately and decided she just might look more at home among this setting than if she were plopped down amid polite society.

"Well, if a bit of reconnaissance tells us Darold is as firmly socked in as you say, he won't have to worry about us this time around." Dane wanted a little more to go on than Cam's say-so.

"He doesn't *look* like a prospector, does he?" Cam's shaken brain brought back that impression. "He had clean fingernails, would you believe?"

"Darold always has had a phobia about dirt." Dane decided preserving the cover story was the best policy. "Think it would have discouraged him from places like this, wouldn't you?" Was that really believable? Dane, Helen, and Cam's fingernails were so encrusted with gunk and grime that it would take each of them a week of scrubbing to make them barely presentable.

"I heard he was once down to his last few drops of drinking water and used it to wash his hands," Helen provided her own embellishment.

"A nasty bunch of people, he and his!" That was Cam's verdict, whether Darold had clean fingernails or not.

"How far up the trail should we start to worry?" Dane had read his charts, but he welcomed feedback from someone who'd been the route before him—if only Cam was reliable.

"It took me most of a day to cover the distance, but I didn't leave the area under any real speed, and I'm still moving at snail's pace. That is, when I'm moving at all."

"Darold leave you any provisions?" Dane didn't see any. Was the plan to saddle Helen and him with this disabled third person that humanitarian good judgment demanded should be evacuated for proper medical treatment?

"I stashed most of my gear before I went in for a closer look."

"We can spare some raisins and walnuts." Dane felt better now that Cam wasn't proving an albatross around their necks. "Unfortunately, we're traveling a bit light ourselves."

"Thanks, but I don't think I'll be doing much chewing for the next couple of days." Carefully, he rubbed his jaw line. "In fact, I should get a move on. You'll pardon me if I'd just as soon not be any-where near you when you, Darold, and Red meet up."

Dane and Helen helped him to his feet.

"You're sure you're okay?" Helen wasn't at all sure.

"Fine, as long as I take it one step at a time. As soon as I reach my stuff, I'll dig in for a couple of days of rest and recuperation. Really. I wish I could be as sure of you two making it as good."

"We'll be okay." Dane knew saying the words didn't make it so.

"We'll back off if it's as bad as you say." Helen hoped they had a chance for retreat if and/or when they made that decision.

"What about a weapon?" Dane's survival instincts had him paranoid, and it didn't seem logical for Cam to feel safe without a gun handy.

"You're bleeding," Helen reminded; Dane's suspicions were catching. "What if a jaguar...?"

Cam's expression brought her up short.

"When was the last time you saw a jaguar?" He even managed a semblance of a grin.

Helen had never seen one, outside of a movie, but saying so would be deceptive in that Cam assumed she'd wandered jungles, claim-jumping, for years.

"Well, I've been in South American wilderness areas a long time, now," he said, "and I've never seen one, either. The main enemies—bugs and bacteria—aren't going to be scared off by my having a gun, although I do have an extra pistol in my cache to replace the one Darold and Red confiscated."

"I guess all that's left, then, is to wish you luck." Helen wished the same for Dane and herself.

Cam shook their hands, said they really should reconsider, and said good-bye when they obviously weren't about to follow his advice.

"What do you think?" Helen asked when Cam was disappeared into the jungle, out of earshot.

"I think we should be mighty careful about our backs. What do you think?"

"He seemed genuine, but.... Yeah, pay close attention to our backs."

They devoted the next two hours to quality trail time. Then, Dane looked for a tree to climb that would provide an overall view of what was only hinted by his charts.

His first selection, by way of a potential climbing pole, had countless clusters of barbwire-like thorns sprouted along its trunk. The second had nasty little ants discovered only when Dane was halfway up. Luckily, the ants had bivouacked somewhere up top and were on their way down, so they didn't manage to cut off his hasty retreat.

Tree three had neither thorns nor ants. It farther surprised with limbs conveniently spaced for climbing. It just went to prove that *third-time-you're-out* wasn't necessarily true one-hundred percent of the time.

Trouble was, some of its higher limbs interlocked with those of adjoining trees to form an elevated net that caught all the leaves and debris dumped from farther up. Digging through that layer of compost was like trying to exit a grave for an unscheduled resurrection.

Once penetration was achieved, although hard-won, the view was worth the effort.

It seemed another ground level: that matting of decaying vegetation punctuated by treetops impressive enough to seem whole trees in their own right. The illusion was of landscape substantial enough to walk on, but any slip through would mean a disastrously long tumble.

As well as treetops, there were up-jutting stone formations. Sometimes vines and vegetation roped these rugged outcroppings. Other times, the miniature mountains denied any rooting on their steep and continually flaking flanks.

Dane saw no signs of major life, human or otherwise. There were plenty of insects. Dane waged a constant battle to keep the bugs from pigging out on his blood *and* on his prolific outpour of salty sweat.

No smoke. No voices. No houses. No telephone lines. No television or radio antennae.

When Dane looked straight down on Helen. He might well have been the only one left on Earth, except he knew better. The enemy was nearby. He could feel them there. What's more, there were probably plenty of them.

Dane would have appreciated a breeze. It needn't have be a cool one, just something to stir up the humid stagnancy of this hole Dan had poked into the world above ground level. However, there was on breeze. There was only blue-to-white sky and a scorching sun.

He headed down, reached for the support of one limb, and spotted the blue-green viper whose fangs were bared to tattoo Dane's arm.

CHAPTER SEVEN

DANE'S REFLEXES TOOK OVER. The snake strike was a blur that provided the serpent a mouthful of air. Serpent scales chafed a portion of Dane's forearm. *Snakes are not slimy,* he would say, from personal experience, from that day on.

The resulting damage wasn't from any injection of reptile toxin but from his spur-of-the-moment jerk-away response that twisted him completely out of balance. He fell in speedy descent before he even knew he was airborne.

The elevated matting of dead leaves, still below him, might have saved him but didn't. It merely concaved with the force of his impact and gave way. Tree limbs conveniently abundant on the way up were seemingly scarce as hen's teeth on the way down.

One short-lived success, a handhold soon lost along with a patch of skin from his left-hand palm, varied his line of fall so that his lower body snagged a branch to cartwheel his ankle into one fork of the tree. The rest of him came to an abrupt, upside-down halt that had threatened to disengage his hip from his leg.

"Dane?" Helen looked straight up at him.

"There seems to be a slight problem." His admission was a breathless reminder that most of his wind was knocked out. "Give me a moment to see if I can take care of it."

He gave it the old college try but without success. The blood that rushed to his head provided uncomfortable warmth and a distortion of vision.

When he admitted, "I believe I do need an assist," Helen was already on her way up. Her dexterity let her cover the distance surprisingly fast, but Dane didn't want her to overlook possible danger in her anxiousness. "Keep an eye out for snakes; my getting out of the way of one is entirely to blame for my decision to assume the *bat* position."

"I hate snakes!" She'd said it at Machu Picchu; she said it now. Saying it here, though, didn't slow her down.

She tested Dane's *locked-in-place* ankle to judge just *how-locked-in-place*.

"The weight I'm giving you to work with is *one-hundred-and-eighty* pounds; anyway, that's what I tipped the scales last time I weighed," Dane said. "Luckily, a loose waistband, as of late, convinces me that my recent experiences have diminished that figure somewhat."

"Nah! You've still a great figure," she insisted.

"Is that blatant female chauvinism, or what?"

Helen laughed, and then proved her banter supplemental to, not replacement for, her assessment of the situation. "Grab hold, why don't you, of that branch you'll find about chest-level, and see if you can manage a handstand that'll allow you to walk your feet up the trunk and out of the fork?"

Dane did as instructed and relieved most of the pressure on his twisted ankle. Simultaneously, Helen used both hands to assist his trapped foot become *untrapped*.

"Coming loose," she assured him by way of warning that he shouldn't let his release put him off balance again.

She made sure he managed a safe turn from handstand to upright position.

The return of blood to his lower extremities left him a little dizzy. Nonetheless, he tested how much weight his ankle would bear.

"Want to give me a damage report?" Helen dropped to the limb beside him.

"The damage is to the memory of my monkey ancestors rolling over in their graves because I didn't retain at least some of the skills they honed in the treetops."

His bout of dizziness passed, and he asked, "Did I thank you?"

"No, but that can be rectified with a kiss." She turned her head and pointed to her cheek.

He obligingly aimed his lips for the spot she indicated but got her lips when she turned back in his direction at the last second. "I learned that trick from Johnny James in fifth grade," she admitted slyly and licked her lips to show just how much she enjoyed it. "The kid was a real pervert, and I shudder to think what he's up to today."

"I'll bet he's not in some jungle, up in some tree."

Helen laughed. Not for the first time, she decided Dane had a marvelous sense of humor. It would have attracted her to him even if he weren't the handsomest, studliest man alive. "Johnny James, eat your heart out!"

They headed down where Dane, once again, tested for damage. His conclusion was that he could hold his own.

"And the view from the top?" Helen reminded him of his objective in the first place.

"No sign of Darold and his friends. Absolutely zilch. If they're dug in, they're burrowed like rats."

They'd done more than *just* burrow, as Dane and Helen discovered farther along the way.

"Trip wire!" Dane warned and automatically extended his arm sideways to keep Helen safely behind him.

The color of the wire in question was mottled to blend with the greens and browns of the ground cover. The long distance it was stretched across the trail made its presence more obvious than had its stretch been shorter. Since Dane had no doubts that it had been set by a professional, its main purpose might well have been more for warning than for maiming. Then again....

"Nasty thing, a M16A1." He'd insisted that Helen maintain a safe distance. "Tripping its fuse makes it levitate a full meter before fragmenting into a million deadly pieces."

It wasn't anything Helen delighted in hearing. Nor was she happy—or, maybe she was—when Dane asked her to stay put while he walked in farther; hopefully, she hadn't pried him from a tree to lose him *or her* to an exploding land mine.

He moved slowly and paid strict attention to his surroundings. As a result, he located, without dying, a PRB-M35, made in Belgium; a PP-Mi-Sb made in

Czechoslovakia; and a French Mk59. This proved that an international company had access to international markets. The age of the mines, 1950-1975, said they had likely seen duty in Vietnam. If anything, their maturity made them less stable and, therefore, more dangerous than weaponry more recently off munitions assembling lines and/or salvaged from more recent battlefields. Their variety assured no easy trace of their last buyer.

Dane prepared for a return to Helen and experienced a chill that had nothing to do with any drop in the temperature. The accompanying warning that rode his gooseflesh and made his hair stand on end was one that had done all right by him in the past. It meant his subconscious registered danger and wanted his conscious to catch up.

He concentrated on a patch of dark shadow a few yards ahead. His pupils dilated to focus all available light.

There was something there! Dane couldn't yet see it, but he could feel, hear, and smell it.

There! All taut muscles outlined in a crouch. Rear haunches prepared to propel.

A jaguar. Leave it to Dane to find one. Expeditions devoted long days and nights to locate this illusive predator and never lucked out. Natives reported it extinct within vast tracts of wilderness. Cam, during all of his years prospecting South America, had never seen a one.

No denying the beauty of the beast. Its deep gold, with irregular splotches of lacquer black, melded perfectly with buttery sunlight scattered among inky shadows. A compact, four-foot body was lengthened by an additional two feet of tail. A good yard across, at its shoulders, it had a large head and massive limbs. This was no harmless tabby.

It drooled syrupy saliva, its jaws wide, its hiss more snake-like than any hundred snakes. It had enormous teeth, eyes maliciously wide, and whiskers stiff and bristling. Its ears pulled back against its head, its flanks shifted, and its tail jerked sporadically at its very tip.

"What a way to go!" Dane contemplated the unfairness as he began a slo-mo reach for his pistol. Of all the things that *could* have killed him, Dane had figured this *liquid-gold-and-jet-black* beast, beady eyes of cold obsidian, admittedly somewhere at the very bottom of the list.

It didn't telegraph its rush, either. It just up and came at him. Dane knew his coordination failed him, even as he completed the withdrawal of his gun, dropped into a low crouch for better balance and to offer himself as a smaller target, and searched vainly for a jaguar suddenly gone. Vanished. Disappeared as if by some trick of illusionists once seen working wild animals on a stage in Las Vegas.

"No way had the cat rushed by or over him. The look in the jaguar's eyes had, without doubt, identified Dane as its next meal.

The man shook his head to clear it and moved his extended gun arm left, then right. His left hand death-gripped his right wrist for stability of aim.

No movement or sound within the parenthesizing underbrush hinted of the beast's present whereabouts.

Dane wiped sweat from his brow and finally spotted the depression in the landscape and almost completely concealed by it. Such man-made holes in the ground had been used for centuries to hunt animals. In guerrilla warfare, they were even used to hunt men.

The dead cat at the bottom was gold and black and red and impaled on three brown wooden spikes.

Dane didn't linger. He couldn't be sure what noises, undetected by him, had been heard by others. There was definite possibility that all the area land mines and traps were monitored. Even now, an alarm might indicate to someone, someplace, that the perimeter was breached, the enemy engaged.

He did a quick about-face and headed for Helen, thankful his experience in the military trained him to remember the placement of already-located booby traps even when approached from the opposite direction.

"Helen?" His whisper forewarned of his return.

She'd heard and seen nothing but quickly read the bad-degree of his ordeal within the uncharacteristic whiteness of his face. Her hand was ready when he took it and guided her toward a nearby pile of jungle-encrusted rock that Dane remembered from his map and from the tree he'd climbed earlier. If they could scale those rocks, they'd have an observation platform from which to view any enemy drawn out by the jaguar's death.

Crossing a slideway of attending scree to reach more solid ground, they caused no more noise than was acceptable in a place where rocks tumbled with obvious regularity.

Steep terraces, next encountered, were less convenient than a natural stairway but were minor obstacles to two people so hyped on adrenaline.

Breathing erratically, they didn't stop until above most of the masking vegetation. They squatted for an even more protected view through a convenient crack in one rock slab once dropped from higher up.

Dane caught the first sign of movement. "There!"

Helen squinted and followed where he pointed. Figures appeared and disappeared through natural rips in the verdant jungle canvas. "It's like trying to figure a jigsaw with only a few pieces."

"Three men. No, four," Dane elucidated. "They're at the pit now." Dane prayed he'd not left any traces of himself behind. "I think one of them is headed down to check out the jaguar."

Helen didn't see it, but *something* was obviously happening.

"The guy's back up out of the hole," Dane continued a few minutes later. "Looks like they're using ropes to haul the cat out."

Helen spotted gold and black. After which, she thought she could tell that the pit was being reconcealed.

"Where'd they go?" Until then, Dane had had them pinpointed through breaks in the forest screen. "Do you see them anywhere?"

"They've entered their tunnel complex." That conclusion wasn't Helen's. She and Dane spun clumsily to confront the speaker whose gun warned, *Don't even think of doing anything silly!*

Dane couldn't believe this guy had sneaked up on them without rattling at least some of the loose stones scattered on the lower slopes.

"Like the North Vietnamese," their captor continued, "they've dug tunnels for everything: kitchen, living quarters, dispensary, rec room, armory, you name it."

"*They*?" Dane was encouraged that the guy at least hadn't included himself within the ranks of the enemy.

"I know you," the gunman surprised. "Sure I do. You're Wilcox. First name: Dane."

"You have me at a disadvantage, buddy." Or, did he? There was something about the man that *did* seem spookily familiar. Dane took a closer look and tried to ring bells of recognition based on black hair, black eyes, slightly off-center nose, and full lips.

"Come on, Dane, old boy! I know I've probably changed somewhat over these last few days, but it can't be as bad as all that. Here's a clue: Who are you and the lady here to pull out of this rat hole?"

The guy *wasn't* a rock sample, and *that's* what Dane and Helen had come for.

"Dayklan sent you, right?" The guy further surprised by putting away his gun, soon to apologize for having drawn it in the first place. "Sorry, but I had to be really sure who you were. I didn't want caught at this point. Not when I've been here long enough to glean some pretty interesting stuff about what and who is down there and what's been done by way of defenses."

"Who exactly are you?" Helen's question was one Dane still needed answered, too.

"What picture did they show you?" he provided another hint. "The I.D. where it looks like I slept on one side of my head too long, my hair standing on end? Or the one from my personnel file that has me in a lab coat, buttons fastened all wrong?"

"It can't be!" Dane protested. Not in denial of the pictures, because he'd seen both of them. There was just no way this guy could be who he insinuated he was.

Dane shook his head. "No way! You're dead!"

"Dead? Check this out." He pinched his cheek. "A very real Roger *K-for-Klinton* Kimlery."

"Impossible!" Helen protested. "I found Roger Kimlery's body. No way do I forget something like that."

"Come on, Dane, tell her."

Dane didn't deny the similarity of this man to the photos Gregory had shown him in briefing prior to Dane being sent to rendezvous with Roger on the mountain. His mind flashed remembrances of that mountain. The darkness. The fog. The beaten and bruised face. The distorting cuts. The draped bandage. Had that been Roger only because Dane had *expected* it to be Roger?

"What are you two trying to pull?" The guy drew his gun again.

"Roger was killed shortly after he passed the stones to Dane at Machu Picchu," Helen insisted. Never having seen photos of Roger, she was the more certain that he was an imposter.

"What do you mean: after *I* passed them? I've got them buried in my hide-e-hole back there." He nodded over his shoulder in indication of where he'd been hidden in order to manage a sneak up on them without warning.

"What if it wasn't Roger at Machu Picchu?" Dane asked. It fit, didn't it? "What if the guy up there was as bogus as his stones were? What if he was sacrificed as easily as all the other victims that The Mentlic Group left scattered along the way to convince us we were carrying the right stuff to Cuzco?"

"Is that possible?" How could Helen know if Dane didn't?

"There would have been no autopsy," Dane mulled. "Gregory would have taken my word for the I.D.; no way would he have laid claim to the body for fear of somehow involving Dayklan prematurely. As far as Inspector Mantáñez, the body would have been a John Doe for speedy burial in a pauper's grave."

"You guys, I'm alive! I'm what you're here for, aren't I?"

"We're here for a second sampling, the first, as turned over by Roger—or by someone who *said* he was Roger—mere chips of basalt," Helen broke the news.

"You're kidding!" He was accusatory.

"What happened to Jim Chimchuck?" Dane tried another line of inquiry.

"They got him, didn't they?" He grimaced at the memory and shook his head. "Never did like Jim. Never. He was so sure that *I* was going to get us caught. *I* was the geologist who didn't know squat about jungle survival beyond what I'd absorbed in one Mickey-Mouse course. *He* was the professional. *He*'d *done* Honduras, Nicaragua, El Salvador, hadn't he! *He* would save us." His laugh wasn't of amusement. "Well, where is *he* today and where am I?"

Dane wanted more of an answer. "Yes, where *is* he?"

"Caught him napping, didn't they! Not literally. I mean, he was awake and complaining when I came down with a bad case of dysentery. He said I would go off one too many times to shit in the bushes and run headlong into the enemy. Being out in the bushes is what saved me."

"Jim knew the *fog-creeping-in-on-little-cat's-feet* greeting/response sequence for passing the stones on the mountain." Dane didn't have to make it a question. Jim knowing would have between Dayklan's insurance if Roger, a mere geologist, didn't make it out but Jim and the stones did. "If Jim knew and was taken, then any interrogator from The Mentlic Group might well have gotten it out of him."

"I thought Jim was a pro." Helen had no qualms about playing Devil's Advocate. Obviously, Dane was the most important person in her life, and she didn't want any mistakes, now, in identifying friend or enemy, that could hurt him.

"They tortured Jim." The mystery man (Roger?) holstered his gun a second time. "Horrible, horrible! They kept using a bullhorn to tell me how they'd stop hurting him if and when I decided to *be a good boy* and come in. Of course, I knew better. They would have killed me, too, right?"

If he needed confirmation, Dane gave it. "Right! What's one more body to The Mentlic Group?"

"Torture or not, would Jim surrender the passwords?" Helen wanted to be sure, and the expression Dane gave her, plus his nod, told her she had no idea how quickly even a professional could break under skillful persuasion.

"I thought I might be able to save him, so I stuck around," Roger said. "I had my gun, and I figured they might slip up and give me a chance to use it. They didn't. There were too many, each with a gun of his own. I finally decided to hightail it on out and make rendezvous. But they were all over the place. Even I was surprised they didn't find me. More than once, they came so close they almost touched me. I would have been a goner for sure if I hadn't lucked out on in finding a small cave in these rocks."

"But they're still looking for you, right?" Dane imagined The Mentlic Group's continued panic with *this* loose cannon just waiting to go off.

"I heard one of them say *he* figured I was dead of exposure. The guy he was with agreed. That doesn't mean that's the consensus of their higher-ups, because every escape route remains covered. I've tried to get out, but I end up back here every time. That's why I was so surprised to see the two of you having gotten this far."

"We're only this far because they know we're here." Dane saw Roger's fear and moved to dispel it. "Not *here,* here. Just *here,* in the general area, nosing around. They expect us to go back to Dayklan and verify the place impenetrable."

"That doesn't get *me* out of here, damn it!" Roger obviously didn't like the picture as painted. "I suppose Dayklan would be as happy to see you two out with the specimens as me returned from the grave with them."

"You're prepared to turn over to us the stones and all you know about the enemy defenses?" Helen doubted she'd be as altruistic in Roger's shoes.

"Only if it means Dayklan will send in a team to secure the area and get me out of here."

"You have enough food and water to last much longer?" To Helen, he looked more emaciated and dehydrated by the moment.

"The jungle provides if you know what to look for," Roger assured. "I picked up a few survival-in-the-wild tips from Jim on the way in. Since then, I've suffered more than one bellyache from my gourmet-dining experimentations, but I'm finding enough to fight off malnutrition. However, I wouldn't recommend Dayklan sit on its collective hands much longer, and not just because I'm anxious to get the hell out of this nightmare. As far as I can tell, there are very few holes left in the enemy's defenses, and someone recently arrived on-site who caused so much back-slapping excitement I'm thinking they plan for him to plug whatever holes remaining."

"He brought in the plutonium." Helen hadn't meant it to be more than a thought, but it slipped out.

"Plutonium, like in A-bomb plutonium?" Roger visibly wasn't pleased to hear it.

"It would have arrived in a protective canister," Dane said. "You have any idea where they would have put it?"

"All I know is that there was a lot of attending activity in and around one specific storage bunker."

"The Mentlic Group would figure it had every advantage if Dayklan came in cold. Pre-knowledge of the exact location of the plutonium, however, might just give any Dayklan assault team the advantage it needs. Therefore, I'd say our best and fastest way to succeed is to get you and your accumulated knowledge out of here ASAP."

"No way do I get let out of here without a fight." Roger's sigh was of disappointment. "That leaves me the alternative of giving you two the blood-red-resolution matrix samples that I've salvaged *and* give you my analysis of the defenses, then pray that's enough to bring Dayklan running to my rescue."

"Easier said than done." Helen expressed her pessimism.

"Unfortunately, she's right," Dane agreed. "You *can't* entrust the specimens to us. Oh, we may be allowed out to pass on the bad news that The Mentlic Group is well-entrenched, but we've no hopes of bringing out the rocks with us. I'd give odds our departure will include full-body searches. I can't help but wonder if The Mentlic Group hasn't hoped, all along, that we'd make contact with you and try to smuggle out the stones in your possession. I've always been uncomfortable with how no one ever bothered to confiscate our portable spectrometer."

Helen saw an additional complication. "Dayklan has already made it perfectly clear that it's not making any all-out effort without first knowing for sure that making one is worth it. Otherwise, it would have sent in an army by now."

"The Mentlic Group isn't going to be nearly as obliging to any Dayklan raiding party, big or small, that follows us in, as it has been, so far, to us," Dane prophesied.

"Why do I not see a rosy picture, here?" Roger asked himself and them. "What would the enemy do if I walked up, specimens in hand, and said, *I'm finished with all this cat-and-mouse bullshit! Have at me*? Do you think that would increase my chances for survival above and beyond anything you or Dayklan can do for me?"

"What about northwest?" Helen had a brainstorm.

"The *direction*?" Dane tried to follow.

"Right!" Helen confirmed but didn't elaborate; her mind milked the possibilities.

"What about it?" Roger was as much in the dark as Dane.

"Jungle, right? Deep wilderness, yes? No towns. No cities. No help. Right?"

"So?" Roger still didn't follow.

"Every time you tried to get out of here, Roger, did you ever head northwest?" Helen asked him.

"Are you nuts? What chances would I have there?"

"Exactly! So, instead, you tried for the river or for the railroad, yes? How many men do you figure the enemy has positioned between you, the river, and the railroad? How many between you and the wilderness?"

Helen took a deep breath to get her thoughts more together.

"Granted, The Mentlic Group likely has men in *both* areas. They'd want to know if a raiding party tried anything *from* the northwest, via parachuting in there. But those watchers won't venture very far a field. What would be the point? And their defensive posture focuses mainly outward, checking for people incoming, not one on the way out. Who in his right mind heads there, right? If you tried and succeeded, there's no one there to help you. Anyway, that's the mentality that just may get you home free."

Roger still wasn't sure what breakthrough Helen figured she'd made.

"Dane and I leave here," Helen clarified, "but we take nothing of interest to The Mentlic Group with us. Not you, not specimens, not any written record of defenses. We throw up our hands and bemoan a nut too hard to crack. We submit to degrading body searches. We profess helplessness and offer begrudging congratulations to the superiority of the clever, clever enemy. We express a desire to get on with our lives. We want marriage. Children. Grandchildren."

She blew Dane a kiss.

"All the while, *you* head northwest," she continued, "because that's the direction no one believes you'd go. Except, we tell Dayklan, once we're out, just where you've headed," Helen capped the plan. "We tell them exactly where to find you, based on coordinates predetermined from the map we give you. Some place not so far away that you can't get there, but not so close that the rescue helicopter is spotted by anyone watching from the perimeter."

"Brilliant," Dane provided his stamp of approval. "Smart girl."

"Actually, it's what the protagonists did in *Beyond Machu*, that romance adventure novel I was telling you about, when they found themselves in a similar situation of trying to avoid a well-entrenched enemy. Only, they had a means of calling in the rescue chopper for all of them, where two of us will have to walk out of here to get one."

"And if, unlike the happy-ever-after ending of some dreamed-up adventure/romance novel, the reality doesn't see The Mentlic Group letting you two out of here?" Roger questioned *their* chances. "I'm game, in that I haven't come this far to surrender, if surrender isn't necessary. On the other hand, my will to live kicked in a long time ago, and I have no intentions of wandering into no-man's land if there's only death there to meet me."

"We set a deadline." Dane said, certainly not sure Helen's plan would work "No one shows within a predetermined time-frame to rescue you, and you do whatever you think best."

"So, where's this map you're going to give me?"

Dane produced it from his jacket pocket.

* * * * * * *

THREE DAYS LATER, Dane and Helen expected Darold at every turn of the trail.

When he did turn up, Helen was more startled than either of the other times; the other times, she'd been made comfortable by complete ignorance.

"Now, don't get excited," he pleaded, "but there's someone in the underbrush who is going to relieve you of your weapons. Don't make this some kind of gunfight at the O.K. Corral."

"You expect us not to be suspicious as to why you'd disarm us?" Dane displayed what he hoped was just the right amount of rebelliousness.

"It's merely a precaution while we have a farewell chat." Darold sounded reasonable. "Do you know there were actually standing orders in some saloons of the Old West that every patron's guns be checked at the door?"

"You're going to surrender *your* weapon?" Helen suggested reciprocity.

He raised his arms in symbol of defenselessness. "I'm completely unarmed as it is. Surely, you wouldn't want the advantage."

"Guess again!" However, Dane slowly reached behind his back; his thumb and fingers brought his pistol around by its butt; the barrel hung toward the ground.

"I don't suppose your friend is going to put aside *his* gun." Helen produced hers in imitation of Dane.

"Even in the Old West, the marshal didn't go unarmed." Darold nodded, and Red stepped out.

"Long time, no see," Red greeted.

"Not nearly long enough no-see," Dane concluded.

"Amen!" Helen agreed.

Red looked sarcastically disappointed but didn't comment.

"This way, please." Darold headed into the jungle on his right. He paused at Dane and Helen's reluctance to follow. "It's only a short way and offers far more amenities."

The large tent, straight from the *Arabian Nights*, was just beyond a stretch of concealing greenery. It filled a section of jungle seemingly cleared, and recently, specifically for it.

Its first compartment contained a table and three chairs. Darold took his chair and waited patiently for Helen and Dane to take theirs.

Red dropped mosquito netting over the door from the outside.

"Isn't this much more conducive to friendly conversation?" Darold insisted. "I can offer lemonade, made with bottled water. There's, also, gin and tonic."

"Once a person dines with Circe, he's reluctant to repeat the experience," Dane observed.

His reference to mythology wasn't lost on Darold who smiled appreciation. "I promise not to change you into porkers *or* drug you, this time."

Helen was tempted to say he was *already a pig,* but she held her tongue. Then, she wondered if just such a retort would have been more in character; she didn't want him to find her acting in anyway out of the ordinary.

"I don't want lemonade," Dane refused. "I don't want gin and tonic."

Helen's throat was dry as a bone. "Ditto!"

"We want out of this place," Dane offered in alternative. "A move we expected would please you and yours only too well."

"Well, we know our hospitality hasn't been the best." Darold showed upturned palms by way of apology. "But we remain curious as to why you've chosen now to go. Say, as opposed to going yesterday or even going tomorrow."

"Maybe it has to do with accommodations that include at least one M16A1, PRB-M35, PP-Mi-Sb, and a French Mk59," Dane suggested.

"All of which you had to suspect would be part of your tour package," Darold reminded. "I told you as much, albeit not in such a specific munitions' inventory."

"There's something to the old adage, *seeing is believing.*" Helen's hoped her voice wasn't as unnaturally high-pitched as it sounded.

"Especially when we watched a jaguar die in a trap set for us," Dane graciously included Helen in his experience.

"Saw that, did you?" Darold sounded as if that might be worth points in their favor. "Nonetheless, do you think Dayklan is going to be satisfied with that as any excuse for you returning empty-handed?"

"Helen and I decided that we didn't want to die, after all, playing corporate war games for corporate profits. Dayklan will have to live with our decision."

"I really wish there wasn't this little voice inside of me that keeps saying you're here with a very big bag of wool to pull over my eyes."

"Look, we are two people sick to death of this place and, yes, frankly, sick to death of you, merely wanting to shed both." Dane wasn't lying on those accounts. "How can that be a threat to you?"

"I'm not sure. My superiors aren't sure. But do you known what I told them, backed by Red?" He didn't wait for a go-ahead. "I said: *Kill them, and we'll be sure we've covered our asses.*"

Dane experienced a definite chill that radiated gooseflesh to his toes from his hairline; he could just imagine what Helen was feeling.

Still, Dane managed composure of speech when he answered. "What did your bosses say to that?"

"Something about the *rules of engagement.* Seems there's this unwritten code of an eye for an eye, a tooth for a tooth. Meaning, I guess, that for everyone of your side that we kill, we can expect an employee from our side to one day prematurely bite the dust. My bosses judged your courier on the train a necessary sacrifice to convince you and Dayklan that you were really running round Peru with the real thing. Killing you now, however, especially when—if—you've come up with zero, could mean a needless future drain of manpower from The Mentlic Group's employee pool."

"*You* don't see it that way?" Helen asked; her voice definitely sounded strained.

"The key wording is, *if you've come up with zero.* I'm not convinced that's the case, and I've survived, thus far, by trusting my instincts. I just don't figure either of you as a quitter."

"I'm not flattered that you think us stupid enough to proceed with something to make us very, very dead." Helen managed a good deal of indignation. "We'd have been fools not to see the writing on the wall."

"Perhaps." Darold leaned back and folded his arms. He didn't look convinced. "If I can't come up with tangible proof that you're holding, I've been instructed to let you go. It's hoped you'll convince your greedy associates that this area is off-limits."

"We can only tell them what we've seen," Dane reminded.

"Just what *have* you seen? Of interest to you, to Dayklan, and/or to us?"

"You want that list of booby traps, makes and models, a second time?"

"I want you both to be completely candid. Something tells me candidness isn't what I'm going to get. So, I must try and remember that I'm merely an employee expected to follow instructions." Darold's smile wasn't attractive. "That doesn't mean that I'm not positioned to take things into my own hands, Red prepared to back whatever my decision. Maybe you drew your guns, and I had to kill you in self-defense. Maybe you made a break for it, and I figured you had something you didn't want us to find. By the way, *are* you carrying out anything you didn't come in with?"

"Nothing but additional disgust toward you and the people you work for." Helen couldn't help expressing her dislike.

"*That* I can live with. Rather, *you* can live with. Anything else, and…" His expression and head-shake indicated prospects not pleasant. "Now, one last time: are you holding something you shouldn't be?"

Helen said, "No," and Dane shook his head in concurrence.

"Stella!"

For Helen, Darold's shout conjured visions of Stanley in *A Streetcar Named Desire*. Except Darold was no Marlon Brando in the role. In *Of Mice and Men*, Darold would have played a rat.

Stella was an unexpected four-foot-four blonde who looked all femininity in her neatly pressed camouflage pants and blouse; she appeared from somewhere deeper inside the tent.

Darold chided their surprise: "You really didn't figure Dayklan the only equal-opportunity employer, did you? In fact, I suggested Stella personally oversee your strip, Dane, while I take care of Helen's." He seemed pleased by Helen's visible shiver. "I pointed out how it would impress upon the both of you the negatives of your involvement in all of this." He got up. "Unfortunately, that idea was vetoed. Don't ask me why. I'm sometimes confused by my superiors' sensibilities in some areas, but maybe that's why they're generals and I'm a mere captain of the troops. I shall compensate by making sure Stella and I are very, very thorough."

Helen shot Dane an *I-don't-envy-you-or-me-this* look; Dane seemed hardly fazed by Darold's threats.

"Through here," Stella instructed Helen, and the two women left.

Dane had undergone complete body searches before, so even Darold's rough and more often than not sexually crude once-over was something he endured with stoic resignation. It was a first for Helen which she'd later report as degrading, humiliating, and not anything she *ever* wanted repeated. Her only consolation was that Stella remained blessedly impersonal, almost mechanical, throughout the whole procedure. To have endured anything even vaguely similar under Darold's probing hands, not to mention his likely ongoing smutty comments in the process, would have been unbearable.

Helen wasn't surprised when she was given entirely new clothes. Stella merely took no chances that anything of importance was hidden in the old ones. Dane, too, was decked out in new duds, and he looked quite handsome when Helen rejoined him.

"You okay?" he asked.

"She's fine," Darold answered for her.

"I'm fine," Helen assured Dane herself.

"Anything?" Darold asked Stella.

"She's clean. Her clothes aren't but, there, I'm only referencing all of the sweat and dirt."

Darold tented his fingers and placed them to his chin as a way of concentration. He dismissed Stella and faced Helen and Dane. "Clean as new-fallen snow, are we? Why am I surprised but not surprised?"

"Because, in our place, you would have tenaciously squirreled away among those land mines until you stumbled over a trip wire and blew out your little pea brain." Dane didn't mean it in compliment.

"Maybe. Maybe." Darold didn't sound insulted.

"What now?" Helen asked a pregnant pause.

Darold's eyes narrowed; his gaze pinned Helen as if she were an insect he was attaching to corkboard. "Now? Now, maybe I call in Red, and we kill you both. Red!" The last was delivered in loud volume.

Immediately, Red appeared through the mosquito netting that hung the door.

"Red," Darold primed, "I was telling Helen and Dane what you and I thought should be done with them now. Would you care to elaborate?"

"Kill them!" Red met Dane's gaze, then Helen's. "Something is rotten here, and it isn't the state of Denmark."

"To think I doubted you could even read, let alone quote Shakespeare." Dane's head shook in feigned amazement.

"I'll think on your recommendation, Red," Darold decided. "In the meantime, walk them to the railroad and make sure they don't meet or talk to anyone along the way. I'll get word to you if you're to slit their throats before any train comes."

As they were herded out, Dane asked, "Helen, sure you're okay?"

"Save the chatter and spare me the resulting air pollution!" Red commanded.

Helen turned to Dane and mouthed, "I'm fine. Really."

She was less fine when they reached the tracks and Red insisted the two sit them dead-center.

Red checked his watch. "Do you know how many people and animals get creamed yearly by stupidly using this right-of-way as a walkway?"

"You're the only one here who takes pleasure in body counts." Dane didn't want the numbers. He just hoped Red was bluffing and that Helen wasn't affected by the jerk's macabre sense of humor. He contemplated how much time he'd have, a train barreling around the bend, to jerk Helen off the tracks, simultaneously putting Red badly wounded either on the other side of the moving train or in its direct path. He decided for sure that was the way he'd have to go, but the air brakes of an oncoming engine began their squeal long before Dane could see them,

170

and long before the engineer could have seen the obstacles in *his* path.

By the time the engine showed itself, it barely moved. It stopped with a good four yards to spare between it and the two people on the tracks.

"Seems someone called ahead and booked passage." Red's wide smile made him downright handsome. This convinced Helen that bad things *could* sometimes come in attractive packaging.

The three, Dane and Helen in the lead, proceeded to the engineer who leaned down to accept a roll of money from Red as blatant payment-in-full for the unscheduled stop.

The train had already begun its spasmodic restart when Helen, Dane, and Red came aboard.

Additional preplanning was indicated by a railway car apparently reserved completely for them; no bathroom smells had kept away passengers, this time around. Red's comment: "Privacy bought in order to blow you both away, without witnesses, if Darold gets word to me to do the deed between here and Cuzco."

Helen's mind insisted she not sleep. Her body, exhausted by the ordeal, overrode her brain, and she dozed intermittently against the hard comfort of Dane beside her. Each time she awoke, it was to find Red disconcertingly leering at her from across the way, Dane offering soothing, "Get some sleep, darling." Each and every time, she was incorrectly convinced there would be no more napping. These might be her last minutes with the man she loved, and she didn't want to snooze them away.

Next time she opened her eyes, her grogginess told her she'd been out for a long time. She was disoriented to find Red gone.

"Red hopped off on the last steep upgrade." Dane gave her a reassuring hug. "Threatening to the very last to blow us both away."

"He's actually gone?" Helen couldn't believe it. "We're actually getting out?"

"It does momentarily *look* that way. So, about this upcoming marriage of ours. The children. The grandchildren."

"Is that an official proposal, Dane Wilcox?"

"Is that an official acceptance, Helen Mallory, or would you rather wait for the engagement ring to make it official?"

"I don't need any ring to make it official." She snuggled closer and enjoyed, as always, the way he kissed her hair. "All I need—all I'll ever need—is you."

"Flattery, my dear," he said, and his fingertips tilted her face so he had better access to her willingly eager lips, "will get you anything; first of all, this kiss."

CHAPTER EIGHT

THEY HONEYMOONED on Martinique at an island estate owned by the Monsbergens; the German industrialist's wife had been one of the first trendsetters to wear Liz Valum clothes, back when Helen's loans kept that designer's fledgling business afloat. Every year, the Monsbergens spent a month in New York, and Liz had made all of the arrangements for the newlyweds who wanted peace, quiet, and seclusion; all of which the estate offered in abundance.

"Oh, but you do taste good." Dane backed Helen against the side of the pool and kissed her again.

"I'll bet a chicken sandwich, green salad, and some cool Riesling would taste good, too."

"Not nearly *as* good," he protested.

"I didn't say *nearly as good*." She initiated a kiss and ran her hands down his muscled naked back to squeeze playfully what she found there. "Just *good*. Tell me you're not just a little starved for something above and beyond my kisses."

"Hmmmmm. Let me think on it, baby, baby."

"While you do, I'll head into the house and rustle us up some grub."

"Wouldn't a phone call to the kitchen do the trick?"

"Did I tell you that I gave Maria and the rest of the staff the afternoon off?"

"How many times does that make, since we've checked in here?" His smile belied even a hint of actual chastisement.

"You're complaining?"

"Am I?"

Another kiss, and Helen pulled herself out of the water. She reached for her terrycloth robe on a convenient chaise longue and, after a brief wave, and an, "I'll be back in a jiff," climbed the low steps.

She entered the house through sliding glass doors that opened on the garden. She had the ingredients for the sandwiches made, except for the mayonnaise, when someone buzzed from the front gate.

The salesman, or whomever, was turned so that she couldn't immediately see his face. This didn't prevent her from saying, "Whatever it is you have to sell, we want none of it."

He looked up into the camera and smiled right at her.

"*You!*" she expressed total abhorrence.

"Is that the best you can offer someone come all this way to bring you a belated wedding present?" Gregory lifted a bulging envelope from his pocket for the camera and Helen to see.

"Did we invite you to the wedding?" They'd had a small ceremony, only immediate family and close friends. The idea had been to get away as quickly as possible for a full recuperation from the traumas of Peru, corporations like The Mentlic

Group and Dayklan, and people like Darold and Gregory.

"Actually, this is your bonus for a job well done. Dayklan always tries to reward its employees for jobs exceptionally executed. So, surely you're going to open the gate for me now."

She did no such thing. Nor did she ask what she just knew he wanted her to ask.

"You're not even the tiniest bit curious for a progress report?" His silly expression said he knew differently.

"I suppose you wouldn't turn down chicken sandwiches, green salad, and white wine if they were offered?"

"I don't suppose I would."

She was tempted to tell him it was a shame none was being offered, but she didn't. "Dane is down by the pool," she said, instead and buzzed him in. "I'll join the two of you in a minute."

That's exactly where she found them a few minutes later.

"Helen? Want to count the additional spoils of our labors?" Dane indicated a pile of large-denomination U.S. bills removed from the envelope and weighed down on the table by a couple of empty glasses.

"If the rest are the same as the ones on top, I'm impressed.

"Dayklan is ever so pleased to have played matchmaker for you two," Gregory said; it was a constant wonder to Helen, too. "I'm, also, pleased to report that as of ten o'clock this morning, Cuzco time, Dayklan has control of the blood-red resolution matrix deposit in Peru."

"Analysis of the samples proved it valuable enough for a concentrated effort to get it, did it?" Helen asked.

"Seems the potential goes way beyond super-conductivity, but I'm not scientist enough to re-member the specifics."

Helen knew it was more a case, now, of need-to-know; neither Dane nor Helen *needed*.

"Speaking of scientists," Gregory moved right along. "One very happy geologist, now back in the States, sends his greeting and thank-you. He was tempted to come along but kept mumbling some-thing about his not wanting to *disturb the lovebirds*. Either of you have any idea what he meant?"

"Have a glass of hemlock," Helen sarcastically offered him some wine. She would have asked for a body count from the successful assault that had oc-curred off in those seemingly now far-away jungles of Peru, but she was eating. She was curious, though, as to whether there really was an eye-for-an-eye, tooth-for-a-tooth mentality that condemned somebody at The Mentlic Group for the courier dead on the train and Jim Chimchuck dead of tor-ture; she didn't ask that, either, though.

She said instead, "I hope I don't turn on the television this evening—" The television hadn't been on since their arrival, and she had no intentions of wasting her time with it later. "—to hear half of Peru is now glowing radioactive."

"Roger's observations proved sufficient for us to avoid that bit of nastiness," Gregory assured. "Brilliant idea, by the way, to send him packing into deep wilderness."

"We thought so." Helen accepted full credit for Dane and her. She ran a fingernail along the length of Dane's bare arm, and he rewarded her with a radiant smile.

Gregory continued, after first clearing his mouth of chicken sandwich, "Kudos for both of you are flying around the Dayklan boardroom, these days. So much so, that...." He purposely took another bite of sandwich to keep them in suspense.

"Don't you have someplace you have to be?" Helen asked over the rim of her wine glass. She could live, thank-you very much, without hearing what else he had to say.

Gregory finished chewing and tapped his lips with the linen napkin Helen had provided. "There's this courier assignment in Paris that begs for a husband-and-wife team. Doesn't the chance for a second honeymoon in *Gay Paree* do wonderful things for the both you?"

"If we'd wanted Paris, we'd be there now. More hemlock?" Helen refilled his glass.

"Really, this assignment is ready-made for the two of you," Gregory insisted, "especially what with you both being between jobs at the moment. Why not supplement your savings while you're waiting for something else to come along? Besides, you work so well together, and Dayklan always has assignments that need a well-coordinated couple who can be trusted."

"I've told United Courier Service never to refer me to Dayklan again." Dane took a bite of his sandwich.

"Yes, that fact did happen to cross my desk, along with a memo from a Dayklan analyst, paid big bucks for these things, who suggested that two people who thrive so well on danger will soon enough tire of a humdrum *normal* existence."

"Don't bet on it!" Helen warned.

"Don't either of you bet otherwise!" Gregory finished his sandwich, drained the last of his wine from his glass, and stood. "Now, if you'll excuse, I *do* apologize for this little intrusion for which I remain confident you'll—one day very soon—thank me."

"Hmmmm." Helen remained doubtful.

They watched him up the steps, where he turned to say: "Be seeing you. In Paris?"

"Do you believe that horrible man has ruined my appetite?" Helen pushed her unfinished plate of food to the center of the table.

"So, maybe we should do something besides eat?" Dane lasciviously suggested.

She smiled coquettishly. "Yeah, maybe we should."

"So what say you to our heading to the house to advantage the present convenient absence of staff?"

"I thought you'd never ask, you sexy man, you." She trailed her fingernail from his naked right shoulder all of the way to his bare and muscled-hard right thigh.

ABOUT THE AUTHOR

WILLIAM MALTESE was born in the Pacific Northwest. He has a B.A. in Marketing/Advertising and spent an honorable tour of duty in the U.S. Army, achieving the rank of E-5.

He started his authorial career writing for the men's pulp magazines and has since penned more than 150 books, both fiction and nonfiction. According to queerhorror.com, this included the first gay werewolf novel ever published. He also has written a number of bestselling women's romances under the name "Willa Lambert" for houses such as Harlequin and Carousel, including the internationally acclaimed Harlequin SuperRomance #2 (*Love's Emerald Flame*), which is being reprinted by Wildside Press along with many of his other novels.

He encourages his fans to visit his websites:

www.williammaltese.com
www.myspace.com/williammaltese